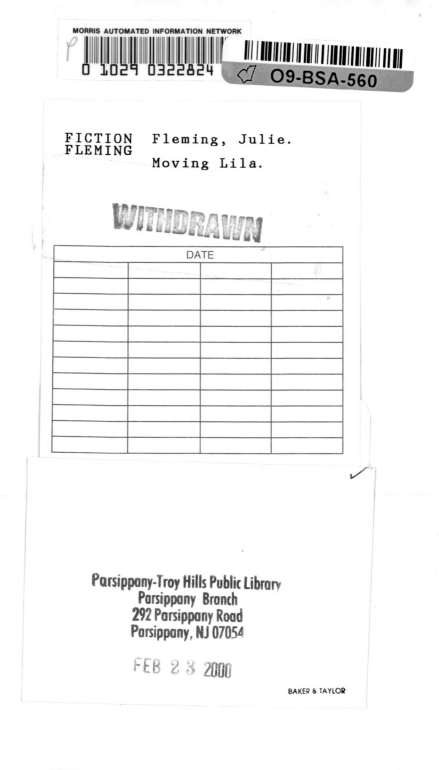

FICTION   Fleming, Julie.
FLEMING
           Moving Lila.

WITHDRAWN

DATE			

Moving Lila

Moving Lila

Julie Fleming

ST. MARTIN'S PRESS

NEW YORK

Library of Congress Cataloging-in-Publication Data

Fleming, Julie
    Moving Lila : a novel / Julie Fleming—1st ed.
    p. cm.
    ISBN 0-312-24409-6
    1. Moving of buildings, bridges, etc.—North Carolina—Fiction. 2. moving of buildings, bridges, etc. Arkansas—Fiction. 3. Inheritance and succession—North Carolina—Fiction. 4. Sisters—North Carolina—Fiction.   I. Title.
    PS3556.I4455   M68   2000
    813'.54—dc21   99-055815
                                                                                           CIP

First Edition: March 2000

10   9   8   7   6   5   4   3   2   1

For John

Moving Lila

One

It was the second Saturday in April. The spring air and light had the feel of outings and tasks and frivolities that she associated with such days. Families drove around in wood-paneled station wagons, fishing poles poking out of cracked windows like toothpicks out of frozen lips. Heads of households filed into Sears in search of washers, filters, studs. Debate Team and Key Club members mazed between vehicles at stoplights, wielding coffee cans, or poster boards for garden-hose car washes in nearby bank parking lots. Dotted lines of cars idled along residential streets, fathers and the elderly waiting while mothers scanned card tables of knick-knacks at yard sales, the earlier the better to find bargains.

That her father, fifty-three and dying of multiple myeloma, would choose this day to read his will aloud to what was left of the family seemed fitting to Mira DeLand. She'd been born on a Saturday, suffered her only broken bone, graduated three times, had her only brush with fame, and written her only suicide note, all on a Saturday, and always assumed that she would die on one. She figured Saturday was her patron day, and when it came around, how she fared depended on its whim.

The drive from Little Rock to Mims, a town whose residents

could and often did all fit in the bleachers of the high school football stadium, was two-lane all the way and had lost its novelty in the eight years she had been making it. An hour into the trip, the knobby hills—afterthoughts of the Ouachitas—faded into flatness and cropland. Along the roadside, crowds of stick-figure pines were replaced by sporadic clusters of silos, branded with family or company names. Quick bursts of wind swirled up off the dry land, turning the air opaque.

Travel grew slower the farther south into the delta she drove, more speed traps, more John Deere rigs straddling the right lane and shoulder, their drivers flooring the gas pedals but still going only thirty. For Mira, any annoyance was offset by their nods and demiwaves. She took these modest acknowledgments of her ant of a Honda to mean, 'Scuse the inconvenience, or All clear to pass, or, when she felt especially generous, We're all in this together.

In early winter, an occasional field would be ablaze, farmers ridding their land of the skeleton of last year's crop. At thirteen, Mira had seen her first field fire on a family trip to the Ozarks. The wind had forced the blaze into a slant so that it cut across their lane. Her mother had admonished her father to veer into the other lane for safe passage, but he'd already begun to do so, saying, "That beats all I've ever seen."

A larger-than-life statue of Shelton Mims, the town's founder, marked the northern town limit. Quarried in the northern part of the state, which was known for that kind of thing, the black marble took on a gray tint with its tiny streaks of white, like marshmallow swirls. Mims's expression was smart and austere, suggesting more reflection than town folklore gave him credit for. The sculptor was local and had made a small fortune from his mail-order business, carving the likenesses of family pets. Mira remembered her mother calling him a no-talent one-man freak show, then striking a look of vindication at the dedication ceremony a dozen years ago. Once the statue was revealed, a murmur had swept wavelike through the crowd as the civic-minded and curious attendees realized that the head was too large in relation to the body. "He should stick to Pomeranians," her mother had said.

A quarter mile from the house, Mira turned onto Duster's Circle, named for a small landing strip and hangar just at the end of the cul-de-sac. The strip was owned by Drop Custers, Inc., whose ads described them as aerial pesticide engineers. Her parents—Wesley and Helen, short for Helena—had gotten a good deal on a duplex, one of only four in the circle, because of the sporadic plane noise. Helen had told the Realtor that that was fine, planes were romantic—*Casablanca* and all that—and they would take it.

At the end of the driveway, Mira turned off the car while it was still rolling. The sight of the duplex—the flesh-toned shutters, the brick, blond and speckled like beach sand—sent a wave of nausea through her midsection, enough to force her eyes shut for a few seconds. After it passed, the twitch in her eye started up again, a recurring thing lately, along with the looming sense that matters were coming around, that there were things to mull over. Her father had gone to great lengths to sustain normalcy since the diagnosis in December. Mira had suggested he join a support group, but he said it sounded depressing, and "Anyway," he had said sweetly, "I've got my own in-house." When she offered to take the semester off from teaching at the university, quit if she had to, he said it was too late, that her name was already on the schedule. Kearney, her older brother by a few years, had offered to quit his job as a bail bondsman, but Wesley said there was too much future in that to quit now. "If you knew you were gonna fall asleep and drown in the bathtub in a year," he had asked one night over chicken-fried steak, "would you just go ahead and draw the bath now?" The trade-off for his "act like nothing is wrong" strategy was that on days like these, when the cancer got top billing, its finality seemed harder to bear.

Mira sat in the car for a minute, one foot on the driveway, and listened to the even tick of the engine cooling off. The two sides of the duplex were like before and after shots in a landscaper's ad. Wesley's was all weeds and overgrown pampas grass, unruly ever-green shrubs webbed with pine needles, mangy patches of saint augustine sod fading into beds of rotten cedar chips. A garden hose snaked halfway into the yard, bulging from water trapped in it by the nozzle.

Rupert Biddolf's half was as groomed as a show poodle. Ru, as he liked to be called, was an eighty-five-year-old retired golf pro who seemed to have redirected his flair for precision from his golf game to yard maintenance. As always, he had mowed in a circular pattern, beginning in the middle to ensure a clean spiral of tracks. The waxy green shrubs that edged his half of the house were trimmed perfectly flat on top, then rounded off gradually toward the bottom to the stem. Topiaries in terra-cotta planters sat on either side of his front porch, each one like three oversized green golf balls balanced on top of one another.

Wesley's unkempt yard was as clear a sign as any that the cancer was having its way. Puttering with the lawn had been as much a weekly ritual for him as churchgoing was for some. Helen, who had died three years ago, had theorized that Wesley's yard-work com-pulsion was just a quiet way of compensating for his lack of asser-tiveness. And to this, he would say, "I like a nice yard is all."

The screen door was closed, the kind with the aluminum silhouette of a woman in a hoop skirt, a man in tails, the two in midembrace. Without knocking, Mira went inside and found her father sitting erect in a folding chair straddling the doorway to the kitchen, a neck stretcher hooked on top of the door frame, the leather harness cradling his chin. For some reason, her eyes shot to his veiny bare feet, flat on the floor and pointed straight ahead, then to an egg-shaped timer balanced on his thigh.

"Lookie here." He smiled as well as he could in his sling. That he had lost more weight was obvious, the way his sky blue zippered jumpsuit looked deflated, not enough inside to give it shape. He looked older, his skin sagging in new places like an ill-fitting glove hastily wiggled on.

Mira set her bags on the floor and walked toward him. He pulled her down by the elbow and she sat on his lap—motions they had gone through a thousand times when she was a child, as much a part of his coming home from work as opening the door. To the cue of creaking sofa springs, she would wander out of her bedroom. With both arms and a grimace, she would pull his boots off, then sit on his strong lap, his legs like tree trunks. As he tapped baby karate chops into her knee, testing her reflexes, she would tell him he smelled like work, and he would tell her she smelled like play. Then from the kitchen, Helen would second that and condemn them both to baths before supper.

Now, his thighs wavered, and to Mira, they felt more like arms than legs. She leaned in to hug him.

When he caught her crying, Wesley skimmed her hair with the hand holding the timer, which ticked in her ear. "Get it over with," he said, his voice grainy and higher than usual, like it sometimes got when he was tired.

From down the hallway, she heard the clap of Kearney's cell

phone closing. He was pushing its antenna down with his chin when he walked in the room.

"Mira, Mira, on the wall." She enjoyed the sweet corniness of his ritual hello. He came over and she stepped up to hug him.

"My two best men," she said, voice garbled. She rubbed her hand against the grain of Kearney's honey-colored stubble. They would never be mistaken for siblings unless you looked at their eyes, and then it would be obvious, the way the green was peppered with spots of brown, the way their eyelids puffed and creased. As a child, she had always wished that they looked more alike. Now, having the same eyes was enough for her, enough of a reminder that they were connected in some out of the ordinary way.

Wesley began dismantling the setup. The neck stretching—Kat, her younger sister by twelve years, liked to call it "necking"—had been a necessary part of his daily routine since a pinched nerve years ago. Mira had always suspected he liked it, though, enjoyed the oddness of the apparatus itself, the way it horrified her friends when they came to the house. She could remember more clearly than she wanted the day Helen had caught Kearney and his shiny-faced, camouflage-clad friend swinging the neighbor's basset hound in the sling. As a punishment, she'd forced Kearney to stretch his own neck for an hour, told him a few dozen times to cut the crap, then sent him numb-chinned to bed with no Tuna Helper.

Wesley reached for a duck-headed cane leaning against the wall—he hadn't needed one when Mira was last here—and walked over to his recliner. There was a kink in his step, an awkwardness that hadn't always been there.

"You look good, babe."

Instinctively, Mira said, "You do, too," then they both smiled, knowing it wasn't true, knowing that the disease had caught up to him. He dug his hands into the armrests and pushed forward, trying to recline. The chair stayed put. He relaxed his arms, then tried again, this time until his elbows trembled slightly and gave way.

"Not too swift." Wesley raised his eyebrows at some imaginary fourth person in the room. Kearney walked over and pulled back on the headrest as Wesley pushed again. Mira had heard the sound a thousand times, the thuddy knock of levers against wood, muffled by velour upholstery.

Kearney and Mira perched cross-legged on the brown shag carpet, a fifteen-year-old remnant from their parents' brown period—brown cars, brown window treatments, all wood furniture, varnished any shade of brown. None of the browns had matched, but they had blended to create the look of a longhaired dachshund's coat.

"Car take the drive okay?" Wesley asked. She nodded and smiled. "Should check the oil before you head back. This heat."

It felt so familiar, the particular tick of the mantel clock, the alternating hum of the refrigerator in the next room over, her father's concern, the way the light from the floor lamp cut his face in half at an angle.

Mira heard the metallic unlatching of the screen door and the sound of flip-flops slapping against narrow feet. It was Kat. "Hey, chickie," she said, nudging her shoes off just inside the door.

"Prom night, is it?" Kearney asked. Kat snorted a sarcastic laugh. She was the summer tour guide at Shelton Mims's birthplace, which meant wearing clothes that could pass as those of a nineteenth-century maid: a full-length flax skirt the color of pecans, white apron, high-collared cotton blouse, hair braided and wound into a tight bun on top of her head.

Kat had come as a surprise sixteen years ago, just as Helen and

Wesley were converting Kearney's empty bedroom into an office. That she'd been unplanned had never been kept from her, this being the decision of Helen, the self-appointed monarch of the family. Kat had been reminded of it a hundred times since she had said her first sentence, and the strategy had worked; it was like this innocuous fact she had grown up knowing, like her date of birth or her mother's maiden name. Kat had taken the news of Wesley's cancer reasonably well. The same had not been true of her mother's death. In that case, Kat had lapsed into a morose low, severe enough to keep her out of school for weeks and, almost mercifully, distract the rest of them from their own version of the same.

Kat kissed her father on the forehead, then went over to hug Mira, who enjoyed the smell of antiques she picked up.

"Close your eyes." Kat brushed her hand over Mira's eyelids. Mira heard the rip of Velcro. "Open up." A few inches from Mira's face was Kat's first driver's license, hard and glossy. Mira smiled and took it for a closer look.

"Glamorous, huh?" Kat flashed her eyebrows.

"As Liza Minnelli."

"It's the lamination," Kearney said, checking a reading on his Casio watch.

Ignoring him, Kat reached for the license. "I made the lady take another one."

"No, you didn't."

"Yeah, I did." Kat took off her apron. "She gave me no warning. I told her to ditch the first one."

"Those damn civil servants," Kearney said.

Kat mimed slapping him on the face, then sunk into the sofa, pulling her skirt up to just above her knees. Though her speech and mannerisms tagged her as a DeLand—the way she pronounced her

double *o*'s and wiggled her jaw almost invisibly when she wrote—
of the three children, she looked the least like either of their parents.
It was as if the twelve years between her and Mira had made Kat
from a different genetic mix. She was fairer than Mira and Kearney,
her hair the color of raw pine, her skin pale—not sickly, but light
enough to burn even on a cloudy day. Though Kat cringed at the
word, she was petite and had the dimensions of a gymnast whose
puberty had cut her career short.

Wesley fingered one of the half a dozen bottles of prescription
pills on the TV tray next to his chair. One of his client's file folders
rested halfway on the tray. Wesley had retired from contracting a
few years ago to start his own business assisting inventors with
prototypes, patents, research, anything they would hire him to do,
really. He had first gotten into the field twenty years ago while
building a home for a fanatic gardener. He came up with the idea
of funneling runoff from the garbage disposal to a compost through
PVC piping that emptied into a shallow aluminum reservoir. The
idea had made him a small truckload of money from a manufacturer and the subject of a feature article in *Organic Gardening*. From
then on, he'd once told Mira, he viewed every bid as a commission,
every bidder as a patron, and every house as an invention.

Mira could tell that her father was fumbling with what to say,
the way he opened his mouth, inhaled a little, then closed it again.
After a minute, he spoke up. "Won't be news to you that I'm on
the downhill slide."

He sat forward in slow motion and glided his bare feet into his
brown corduroy house slippers lined with faux fur. He had had the
same pair long enough for the soles to be worn to a slant because
of the way his feet bent slightly toward the outside as he walked. A
dozen times Mira had heard him tell the story of Louis XVIII, who,

en route to his Belgian exile in the middle of the night, had said, "What I regret most is the loss of my bedroom slippers, for they had taken the shape of my feet." Wesley's fascination with the French Revolution was either because his mother was French—her maiden name was DuChaillu—or because he had been told more than once that he resembled Napoléon; Mira had heard him offer both explanations. Whichever the case, they had had pets named for royalists, theme parties requiring everyone to come as their favorite revolutionary, and crêpes suzette every Bastille Day for as long as she could remember.

Her father picked up a manila envelope from the rolltop desk on the far side of the living room. He pulled out four envelopes and handed one to each of them. The will was on two sheets of unlined legal-size paper. The top of the first page read, "The Last Will and Testament of Wesley Chester DeLand," then subheadings: "Revocation," "Marital Status," "Residuary Estate," "Special Gifts," "Special Instructions." The executor was listed as Jack Scanga, his lawyer.

"No need in postponing this," he said. The putter of a crop duster got louder as it descended to the airstrip nearby. He sat back down in his recliner, let the cane fall between his legs, and looked first at Kearney.

"The business'll go to you, Kearn. The income's modest and sporadic, I know. It'll be a supplement is all." As Wesley held his copy of the will, his hands shook, one of the side effects of the drugs. "You'll get fifty percent of whatever profits there are. The other fifty'll go into trust for Kat's college." He shifted his eyes to Kat. "Babe, when you're done with school, same will go to you directly."

As their father spoke, Kearney held the bridge of his nose between two fingers, eyes clamped shut, head bowed toward his lap;

Kat listened, her arms pressing her legs to her chest; Mira kept her eyes on the whirring ceiling fan as she hopelessly tried to keep track of a single blade.

"Course the savings, what there is of it, will be divided between the three of you. Kat, yours'll be in trust until you're twenty-one. As for the duplex, you all can decide what to do with it. If you need it to live in, or if you decide to sell it. Ru's even hinted he might buy it as an investment. I can live with any of those." Catching what he had said, he lowered his head with a faint smile.

A three-second electronic buzz came from the direction of the mailbox outside, signaling the mail's arrival. The matchbook-size device was his most recent invention. He had sent letters and sketches to high-end trinket companies that catered to crafty men with surplus capital, and on a last-minute whim, he had sent the same to the postmaster general. He was still waiting on a request for a prototype, or a meeting—anything.

He mumbled that he would get the mail later. Then, with his head still aimed down at the will but his eyes raised a notch to meet Mira's, he said, "You get Lila."

Lila was a house they had left in 1979, more then seventeen years ago, a house in Ona Island, North Carolina, at that, and Mira figured that under normal circumstances, it would be no more than a family footnote, skimmed over, all but ignored. That they avoided talking about it should have meant there was nothing to say. That Kat had never even seen the house and knew next to nothing about it should have meant there was nothing worth seeing and nothing to know. But there it was, like a first coat of paint, always threatening to be exposed. Wesley had designed and built the house. He adored it as if it were his child, though Mira had once been shrugged off as melodramatic for saying so. No one in the family recalled why the house was named Lila, only that it had been as long as they could remember.

Rattling the few pills left inside one of the bottles, Wesley went on: "But I want you to be responsible for moving it to Mims." Mira waited for a punch line, some qualifier, but the stare stayed even, his voice as cool and detached as an estate attorney's. "The cost'll be covered by the savings. I want it to go on the county land." He had bought the fifteen acres just outside of Mims three years ago, soon after her mother died. "You can live in it, even rent it out, far as I'm concerned. Just keep the DeLand name on it."

Mira tried to picture the house as it might appear now, but she could only come up with a vague outline. The exact look of it had faded, like the features of a friend you haven't seen in a long time. She glanced at her brother and saw her own expression in his, a hard stare straight at their father, a look of calm shock, if there can be such a thing. She put her hand to her eye to stop the twitch. She could feel it under her middle finger like a pulse.

Wesley folded his copy of the will in perfect thirds, pinching the creases between two fingers. "Those are the big things, I guess." He leaned back in his chair as if waiting for a rebuttal.

"You haven't signed it yet?" Kearney asked.

"I wanted to okay things by you."

"None of this matters." Kearney thumped a knuckle against the will. "You've got our okay." He looked to Mira for support. She shifted her eyes to the carpet, parting strands so she could see where they were woven into the backing, like a dog's fur into its skin.

"Seems like that now." Wesley crossed his legs and pressed a hand between his thighs. "But these won't be minor details once I'm gone."

"It doesn't matter," Kat told him.

"It will" was all he said.

By midafternoon, Mira and her father were alone in the house. Kearney had gone to bail a counterfeiter out of jail, saying he would ask the guy to take a look at Wesley's livre note, supposedly autographed by the Marquis de Lafayette. Kat had gone for peaches at Rhonda's #6 Fruit Stand—any excuse to drive.

It was Wesley's least favorite time of day. The newspaper read, the mail opened, too late for coffee, too early for the drink he had sworn off anyway, the day seemed at its lowest ebb. From the living room, he could tell by the shadows that the afternoon's swollen clouds were moving slow and big like blimps across the sky. He had fallen asleep in his recliner to the crackle of a Depression-era movie on TV, then woke up to the sound of boiling water.

He found Mira in the kitchen peeling tomatoes for marinara sauce, dipping each in the steaming water for a few seconds to loosen the skin. She stood with her back to him, all weight on one foot, the other foot cocked behind her ankle. She wore a patchwork sundress that showed off the flawless posture she had inherited from her mother. Her pecan brown hair was twisted into a loose bun on top of her head and secured with a State Farm pencil. She would never not strike him as beautiful.

"Are those the scalps?" Wesley pointed to the pile of discarded skins on the counter.

"Yum."

"So how are you with all this?"

"All which?" Mira asked.

"Moving Lila." His eyes drifted to a wooden plaque resting on the windowsill, HEL'S KITCHEN etched in cursive.

"Funny how I believed you when you said the land was an investment."

He arranged the peeled tomatoes in a circle on the cutting board. "That was true."

"Just incomplete." Mira jutted out her perfect chin, one that Helen had always taken credit for but that he thought looked more like his own.

"Kat's been dying to go there, asking questions, says she's got a right to see it. Whatever, we can't let her close to that." Wesley remembered telling Kat the half-truth that they had left because he was offered a job at a contracting company in Mims, nothing about Helen's affair with the Reverend Joseph Bleecher. "If she goes there, she'll dig your mother up."

"And you don't think bringing Lila here is gonna run the same risk?"

"This is not a whim." He twirled an index finger in small circles. "She just can't know."

"Let me fester on it for a while."

He barely scratched figure eights on Mira's upper arm. Her goose bumps came out on cue. "Fester away."

 *Two*

As May approached, the indecision of spring leveled off into the damp swelter of summer, her father's red blood cell count fell, and everything Mira felt and every decision she made seemed magnified in intensity and importance, as if the whole ante of her life had been upped. Wesley had always loved summer, his kindred season, he said, so privately she thought that if he had to die, that's when it should happen.

After the weekend of the will, back in Little Rock, Mira spent the next week frazzled and making plans to be gone for the summer. She was finishing her first year teaching city planning at the university and didn't expect any resistance when she reneged on the summer classes she had agreed to teach. The chair of the department, a sweet man around her father's age named Dick Bratigan, told her to take as much time as she wanted, asking only that she write a letter to the dean explaining the need. The dean was a flashy administrator type, liked to say "proactive," claimed to be an empowerer of the faculty but rarely was seen mingling with them. So Mira didn't expect anything different from what she got: the original copy of her own letter, which read with the objective dryness of an obituary and gave as few details as one, sent back to her through campus mail, "Leave granted. Take care" scribbled at the bottom.

There were precedents. Marcus Sheetz, the department's cartographer, had done the same two years earlier to get divorced. When things started up between Mira and Marcus in the fall, she'd learned about the ugly details—namely, his wife's affair with their postal carrier. Marcus said he had seen it coming, suspected something was up when the mail started arriving before he went home for lunch, then knew he had been right when he found a man's Lycra knee-high in the foyer's ficus tree. His wife came clean a week before their first anniversary, just a month before they had their first child. In the divorce that followed, one bone of contention was the paternity of their son, which was determined by DNA testing. Marcus didn't know whether to be devastated or relieved when he was told by his lawyer that the baby was not his and that at least this would make fault in the divorce easier to determine.

Mira finished the semester in a semidaze, skipped out on end-of-the-year functions—the Faculty Appreciation Luncheon, the vice president's retirement reception, the Student Grievance Committee's spring mixer—and developed a flair for truthful but vague answers to questions about her time away. She couldn't quite fathom that the family stuff might be over in a few months, that things might be resolved, the reassuring monotony of teaching resumed. Too many things had to happen between now and then for any of that to seem real.

She spent her last day on campus sorting through discarded piles of papers on her desk: essays students had never picked up, interoffice memos, revised policies and procedures, minutes of meetings she should've attended. She had lucked into a prime office on the third floor of Stampey Hall, one wall made completely of glass for an uninterrupted view of Little Rock's asymmetrical suburbs. She had been hired quickly to replace a senior faculty member in planning who had died just before the start of the fall semester. His next of kin, distant cousins, had never claimed his stuff, so all of it stayed: computer files; graduation regalia from the University of Kentucky; a shrine to Amerigo Vespucci; a stash of condiment packets; an old tabletop globe, the skin peeling in the northern hemisphere. She hadn't yet gotten over the creepiness of these leftovers.

Mira heard the familiar sound of boots clogging unevenly against the institutional linoleum. It was Marcus. Just before he came in, she put her hand to her forehead, fixed her stare on a memo, tried to strike a look of being overwhelmed. He stopped in the doorway, which only topped him by a few inches, and leaned a shoulder against its frame. She had always loved his lankiness. He smiled, arms folded, and said, "Miss, um, can I get my grade?"

"Hello, Marcus." She smiled back, hoping for just small talk. He sat down in the chair across from her desk. "All done?"

"I'm due a few more sexual favors before I turn in grades."

"So you made it to Navin's workshop." Navin Neihart was a former faculty member who had given his eighteen year old flame an *A* in world geography and was only found out the next semester when her Russian geography professor discovered she didn't know latitude from longitude. Tenured and all, Navin Neihart was fired and went on to become a wholesaler of cardboard boxes.

Marcus kicked at the air with the toe of his boot. "I was the facilitator."

Mira tried to mimic Kat's lovely snort of teenage sarcasm, but it came out only as an exaggerated inhale. As if to rescue her, Marcus changed the subject in a hurry. "So what are you teaching this summer?" He asked this with a smirk and a forced raise of his eyebrows. He had heard she was leaving and was trying to get a squirm out of her.

Whatever existed between them wasn't something that would be devastated by a few months apart. The first time things had become amorous was on a trip to the American Planning Association Convention in New Orleans last October. After a day of sessions on antisprawl laws and context-sensitive signage, Marcus and Mira had left the passed-out planning majors in the hotel and taken the school van for a ride, careful to peel the magnetic logo off the van's side. They drove around for a while in the crevicelike streets of the French Quarter, then parked by the river and joined the loiterers. A bronzed patriot they had never heard of barely hung on to a bucking horse, front hooves in midair. Mimes stacked pennies, dimes, and quarters on park benches, their painted white skin glowing in the shadows. Panhandlers nudged their coffee cans toward them but said nothing as they passed, all this to the smell of pot and urine.

It was over beignets, in the milky light of the overflow benches at Café DuMonde, that Marcus had asked Mira if he could kiss her—before doing so—which at the time she thought was the most romantic thing he could've done. It was a sweet moment, but soon everything leveled out into a lethargic, low-maintenance arrangement, absent declarations of love, which seemed to be working out fine for both of them.

"I was going to call you before I left," Mira said, and this was true, but only because she didn't want to leave any messes that would have to be tidied when she got back. Marcus was harmless enough, but his "damn, I'm good" attitude—which she could find both ugly and appealing, depending on how he carried it off—had the effect of making him seem like an automaton, deadened to pain, emotional or otherwise, and Mira knew that if she left without tying things up with him, it would do more to his conceit than any feeling he had for her. Even so, she wouldn't need the hassle of soothing a damaged ego when she came back.

"Anything I can do?" he asked. Because it seemed so genuine, this bit of concern caught her slightly off guard.

"Ask me that three months from now."

Marcus reached for the corner of the desk and picked up a Magic 8 Ball. He rolled it twice between his palms.

"Will Mira be on the fall schedule?" He turned the ball with the window facing up. " 'In all likelihood.' " He paused and let his head fall back. "Will Mira suffer from memo withdrawal this summer?" He rotated the ball, then read the answer: " 'Chances are slim.' "

Mira smiled. "That was a tough one."

"You ask one."

"Will Marcus find someone else to go to the dog races with?"

Marcus rotated the ball, then read the reply: " 'Chances are good.' " He smiled and patted himself on the chest.

"Hand it over." Mira reached across the desk. "Will Mira come back to Little Rock?" She tossed the ball up, caught it, then waited for the bubbles to settle. The triangle read "Not likely," but for no good reason, she said, "It is certain." Marcus crossed his legs and leaned forward with his forearms on his knees.

"I'll count on that." Marcus got up from the chair. Mira walked around the desk and gave him a one-armed side hug. He always smelled good, she would give him that.

"I really was going to call you."

Marcus smiled and ambled out, waving over his shoulder. She sat down at the desk and went back to the 8 Ball.

"Will my clutch make it to a hundred and fifty thousand miles?" The reply: "Not likely."

"Should I move the house?" She felt silly but rotated the ball anyway, then waited for the triangle to right itself. The answer: "All signs say yes."

She dialed her father. It took him six rings to pick up. "Hello?" he answered.

"Remind me to give you my cordless phone."

"Where are you, babe?" His voice sounded mechanical and remote, as if his batteries were low.

"Puttering around at school." She started undoing a paper-clip chain. "I'll be home day after tomorrow."

"What about your apartment?"

"I've talked to my landlord. He's gonna keep an eye out."

"Don't forget to stop your newspaper."

"I'll be home," Mira said. "Love you."

"Love you," he answered to the background of a plane's sputter.

 *Three*

Wesley lived ten May days after Mira said her clumsy good-byes for now to Little Rock and made the drive back to Mims, one she would always associate with the cancer, every land-mark now a doomed reminder of it. The doctors—he had seen several recently, including one who had myeloma patients state-wide—had given up on treatment. When first diagnosed in Decem-ber, he had already been in stage three. The cancer was pervasive, its cells in his bone marrow, the lesions on his ribs and right femur. It had taken over like kudzu, the most recent doctor had told them: "It'd be like treating pneumonia with Vicks salve. Or a broken leg with an Ace bandage." Kearney, who had gone with Wesley to the appointment, had cornered the doctor alone and admonished him for throwing around whimsical descriptions of the cancer. They had conveyed more doom and gloom than he thought anyone needed to hear.

For Mira, the creepiness of moving back into her old bedroom, even for the time being, wasn't lost on her. The room had gone untouched. Her mother's plans to install a ceiling fan, a bay win-dow, a valance—all that had come to a halt with Kat. Mira's trundle bed had been replaced with a double for guests, but her collection

of 45s—the one on top by A Flock of Seagulls—the turntable, the
Lincoln-Douglas debate trophies, the Snoopy latch-hook rug, the
bad high school art, a unicorn calendar from 1983—all this remained, like a time capsule opened too early, an embarrassing
shrine to her adolescence.

More than anything, the room called up what she could remember of the one she had shared with Kearney in Ona Island, the way
its ceiling sloped almost thirty degrees—A-shaped, like a bird-
house—complementing the room's only window, a triangular one
on the wall opposite the door. The window was just a foot below
the ceiling, high enough so that she couldn't see ground level, just
the sky and tips of the highest pine trees, like a window in a jail
cell. It faced east, so the sunlight filtered in early, drenching just a
slice of the room with blond light, spotlighting knots in the hardwood floor and weightless clouds of dust. As the morning faded
into midday, less and less light would make it through. By mid- to
late afternoon, the room would sink into a pale, then dark blanket
of blue that had always given Mira the sensation of being in an
aquarium. She still imagined each change in light as a mood the
room passed through, a patterned sway from joy to confusion,
boredom, or whatever.

Such a sense of normalcy prevailed those last ten days of Wesley's
life that Mira's outlook on how long he could keep it up improved.
He wouldn't have noticed, though, because all along she had acted
under the assumption that he was on the mend. She had never
forgotten one of her college professors, who, in the middle of a
lecture on the origins of World War I, had said, "Regarding the
question of free will—whether we have it—this is my view: We
must assume that we do." Mira couldn't remember how this con-

nected to the war, only that she was struck by it in some nineteen-year-old way.

She wanted to think that her own outward optimism had influenced Wesley when he scoffed at the doctors who told him to stay in the hospital bed that they had insisted he rent. "One slip and you'll have two bones for every one," the same flippant doctor had told him. Ignoring this advice, Wesley had insisted on sticking to the wheelchair, even sleeping in it, despite the fact that the second day Mira was there, he woke up with such a severe crick in his neck that he couldn't turn his head, not even a little. She tried to dissuade him, but he came back with an elaborate rebuttal. "Sitting up is more conducive to respiration," he said. "When you're lying down, the blood flow's more likely to stagnate." He held his arm out to illustrate. "Take the Mississippi, the way it just skims along like it's not in any hurry. Then imagine turning it on its head, hanging it from the sky." He turned his forearm perpendicular to the floor. "The water would flow so fast, with so much determination and heart, the jetlike pressure of it would carve a canyon in the ground the size of a small city."

Thinking he was only half-serious, she said, "How long did it take you to come up with that, Dad?" But the way he stood his ground, saying nothing, just looking back at her with his watering chocolate-colored eyes, it seemed to her like the most rational thing in the world, and the next day she wheeled the hospital bed into the corner of his bedroom, out of the way.

And so, every night, she followed him—he preferred to wheel himself—to the bedroom, where he would reverse his chair flush against the wall. At his request, she had nailed a pillow into the sheetrock to meet his head as he leaned back. On his nightstand, within reach, were his pills and water, which the doctors told him to drink constantly for his kidneys. For lack of a bell, she had borrowed a harmonica from Kearney's leftover things—he had gone through that phase in junior high—to leave by Wesley in case he needed something in the night.

He seemed to get a second wind every night just before he went to sleep in his wheelchair, head propped up, blanket draped over the chair and tucked behind his shoulders. He said it was the sleeping that scared him most, and that talking calmed him, made him less likely to fight it. So it was there, after a good day, when he had seemed to feel strong, that Mira brought up the house.

"Kat's been asking if she can make the trip with me."

He shook his head in slow motion. "A bad idea."

"Maybe, but it seems like questions from her are inevitable."

"You're right there. All the more reason to bring it here rather than have her go there."

His eyes were focused on Lila's diazo blueprint, the size of a poster, hanging just above a dieffenbachia plant on the opposite side of the room. After his wife died, he had had it customized in a cherry beveled frame and nonglare glass. The blue lines seemed to have bled, veining out into the onionskin paper. The dimensions of the small house, the circumference of the pipes, the depth of the rooms, the position of every stud, the angle of every slope, the width of every doorway—all of this was labeled, numbered, specified, like a page from da Vinci's notebooks.

"Moving the house within her reach isn't gonna soothe her curiosity," Mira said.

"It's not the house I'm worried about," he replied. "It'll be different here."

"How's that?" Mira adjusted the wheelchair so he could

straighten his legs. "You move a python from a rain forest to a nursery school, it's not gonna shrivel up and die."

He flashed her a condescending look that even Kat would've envied. "It's a house, babe." He switched off the lamp at his side. Only a slice of light came in from the hallway. "Anyway, I want the house here." This last bit seemed thrown in, as if he hadn't planned on saying it. He was swirling a cup of water in tiny circles. "It's just one trip back, to oversee things," he said. "Jack can help you make the arrangements."

"What about the fact that Mom wouldn't want this?"

"She'd want Kat to know about the affair even less. Anyway, what happened there's her fault." She loses, he was saying, but in gentler terms.

"What if I said this was selfish?"

"Why can't a dying man be selfish?"

And Mira knew there was no way to argue with that.

If Kat had known about their tiptoeing around, she would have started in on how if she could drive, she could handle this; if she could watch movies with adult situations, she could handle them in real life. But then, how would she know about real life, anyway? she would throw in. And once they had filtered the sarcasm out of what she had said, they all would have known that she was right, which would have helped to prove her point in the first place. When Mira thought about the insecurity and clumsiness of her own sixteenth year, she wondered where Kat got her even head. More than anything, she was glad for it, because it was her even head, or maturity, or whatever, that made them both forget that twelve years separated them. They still felt like sisters.

The only time Mira saw Kat cry before their father died was one midnight when she got up to use the bathroom. Mira picked up the hum from the hallway and the faint blue glow of the computer in the living room. She found her sister in front of the terminal, looking slight, head pointed up toward the screen. She was crying, wincing a little, her face curled up at the cheekbones. As Mira walked toward her, faint creaks came from the floor, muffled by shag. Kat swiveled to face her.

"Come see," she whispered. Mira squatted beside her. On the screen was a business letter from Wesley addressed to Spence Hoenig, one of his clients.

Dear Spence:

I hope this letter finds you and yours well. When we last spoke, I informed you of the interest of Fenny Industries in your in-home recycling system. I believe we confirmed your meeting of July 15. You will be given a maximum of thirty minutes for a presentation. Good luck with it.

Since last we talked, a change in plans for my business has been firmed up and signed to legally. My son will soon be managing the company. He shares my own fascination for the field and will carry to fruition the plans that you and I have in the works. He will contact you soon. Until then, please let him know if you have any questions.

All Best,
Wesley DeLand

Tears had pooled in the small cavities just under Kat's eyes, reflecting the blue of the screen. She held up an open folder. Mira thumbed through the stack of a dozen or so letters inside, each ending with the same news. The one on top was addressed to a photographer in Key West who had contacted Wesley after seeing his ad in *Omni*. She had developed a screen that fit over the lens of a camera, invisible on finished pictures, to prevent fingerprints, dust, and water from reaching the lens. Wesley was sending news of an investor.

The screen saver kicked on an endless spray of asteroids. Kat nudged the mouse and the file reappeared. "Kearney's been trying to talk to me about heaven and stuff." Kat paused and stared hard at Mira, as if waiting for her to confirm or deny its existence.

"I know." Unsure of what she was claiming to know, Mira was more surprised than anything, since Kearney mentioned his religion about as often as he did his blood type, or shoe size, and with about as much gusto.

"Helps to know Mom's there waiting for him, like she always was," Kat said.

If Mira had closed her eyes right then, just listened to Kat's voice, some floaty, childlike quality that it had never lost, her sister could've been seven years old, Mira a flustered nineteen-year-old, fumbling around for the adult thing to say.

As it was, Mira left them open, and she was twenty-eight, but all she could come up with was, "Yes."

The next night, after her father and sister had gone to bed, Mira found Kearney on the couch with a week's worth of newspapers at his feet; he didn't subscribe at his home. He was reading the local police blotter.

"What's the skinny?" Mira leaned against the opposite end of the couch so that she faced Kearney, their feet overlapping in the middle.

He folded the newspaper backward and pulled it closer to his face. "Your basic parole violations. Twenty-year-old female slapping kid with wire brush. Eagle Scouts linked to rash of dead frogs in mailboxes."

"They were trying for their misdemeanor badge." She tossed two back issues of *Christian Word* onto Kearney's stomach. "There's your contraband."

Mira could remember five years ago when Kearney had visited her at grad school and told her he had retaken to religion, the only member of the family to do so, despite their mother's insistence that they leave it alone when they left North Carolina. Until then, they had been lazy members of Success Baptist Church in Ona Island (an island was nowhere to be found, but the town founder's wife, Ona, had always wanted to live on one, according to the folklore). But on their way out of town, Helen had mailed a letter to the Southern Baptist Convention demanding that the family's membership be withdrawn. Kearney, then, had to be underhanded about his churchgoing, even after their mother died, because no one wanted to put Wesley in the position of deciding whether to condone something his late wife would have condemned. And since their father had a habit of dropping by Kearney's house, sometimes checking the mail as a favor as he pulled in the driveway, Kearney had subscribed using Mira's work address. So when she saw him on occasional weekends, his copies of *Christian Word* were layered between her clothes, to be slipped to him in some quiet corner of the house when no one was around.

"So how'd it go today?" she asked. He had set the afternoon aside to talk to his father about the business. They had planned it for when no one else would be home, not because of any confidentiality, Mira figured, but because there would be talk of Wesley's being gone soon.

"Bailed out a woman caught smuggling her better half's semen out of prison so she could get pregnant."

"How'd she manage that?"

"Beats me." He laughed silently, his stomach jiggling up and down. "Call her up and ask her."

"And that's worth an arrest?"

"No conjugal visits in Arkansas. If you get married, commit your crimes in Mississippi. They allow 'em."

"I'll file that away," Mira said. "I meant, how did things go with Dad?"

Kearney let his head fall back against the arm of the couch, the paper resting on his chest. "He gets so invested in things, works himself up."

"Expects the same from you, I guess."

"I'm fine with the business. It's the house thing that's gonna be spooky."

"Did you say anything to him?"

Kearney was stretching a rubber band between two index fingers. He flashed her a confused look. "What would I say to him?"

"That moving the house here's gonna get to you."

"It doesn't matter what gets to me. Not bringing the house here is not an option." The rubber band popped and shot silently into the carpet. Then, as if he knew what she had in mind, he said, unflinching, "This isn't the kind of thing you can renege on."

The closest thing Kat had to a good-bye with her father was the next day, which was two days before his death, as it turned out. She found him in the dining room, his chest flush against the table, his chair wheeled underneath. She stood unnoticed in the doorway behind him. He had emptied the antique cherry liquor cabinet devoted to Napoléon-related books and artifacts, the house's only sanctuary. On the table lay his entire French Revolution collection, arranged into three groups. She recognized most of the stuff. The bust of Josephine Bonaparte, three or so inches tall, wood varnished the color of chocolate. A framed lock of Maximilien Robespierre's lightish hair, which Wesley had ordered from a dealer. An 1804 silver franc bearing the profile of Napoléon as first consul and chopmarked from Asian trade so merchants could judge the quality of the metal. A postcard from present-day Elba. A laminated reproduction of the Declaration of the Rights of Man. A Marie Antoinette salt and pepper set, her torso full of pepper, head full of salt. A biography of Dr. Guillotin, inventor of the decapitation device he thought to be more humane than quartering.

Wesley held on his flattened palms the livre note autographed by the Marquis de Lafayette, sheathed in a clear plastic envelope. He sat there staring, just barely nodding his head for what seemed like several minutes. Then he reached for his inventory list and made a notation next to one of the entries, wiggling his jaw as he wrote. The loops and dots of his pencil swished and ticked into the oak table underneath. Then, the notation made, he put the livre note in one of the groups.

It was when it occurred to Kat that there was a group for each heir that she felt the creeping burn of nausea and tears.

He picked up an original painting of Olympe de Gouges, the forty-five-year-old playwright who had tried to be excused from the guillotine by claiming pregnancy. She had been beheaded only after declaring, "Oh, Liberty, what crimes are committed in thy name." He held the place mat-size portrait a foot from his face, looking back and forth among the three groups. Then from behind, Kat could see the sides of his face constricting, his head lowering slowly, as if by a pulley, into his hands. She moved up behind him and pressed her face into his neck, which felt warm. He pulled her to his side and she knelt. The crying was so familiar now, as natural as breathing.

After a minute of this, he pulled her chin up in his hand. "I'm not as fragile as your mother believed."

Two days later, when Mira found him sitting erect in his wheelchair without a pulse, his head cocked back at an angle against the pillow, the shock wasn't lessened by the warning they'd had. The funeral was small and there were remarkably few arrangements to make, since Wesley had taken on that task before he got too sick to do so. He was buried next to Helen. The tombstone he had chosen for her foretold of his own death three years before it came, the dash that followed his date of birth emphasizing that it was only a matter of time. He had opted—eerily, Mira thought—to have their wedding photo displayed behind a thick plastic oval on the stone. The shot was a close-up, just wide enough to reveal the high neckline of Helen's ivory raw silk dress and Wesley's black satin bow tie. Her mother's too-wide smile revealed a chipped bicuspid that Mira had forgotten.

They had to settle for a 5:30 P.M. graveside service. "Saturday's the choice day for funerals," the director had told them. Amid the smell of fresh dirt and ten different rings of flowers propped up on tripods, Mira thought of her father's promise to her mother to leave certain things behind, how it was being thrown by the wayside, and how the responsibility would shift from the one who had made the promise to the one who had failed to carry it out. She thought of the sun setting over Lila, the bedroom with the sloped ceiling succumbing to the dark blue light, maybe today lapsing into sentimentality.

 *Four*

In the top left corner of Jack Scanga's business card, his glossy face, in color and slightly raised off the paper, floated over the scales of justice. Mira was calling to see if he could meet with her on short notice. He said he had appointments all day but that she could come by at noon, if she didn't mind watching him eat.

Wesley had retained Jack Scanga years eariier when a customer threatened to sue over faulty ductwork. He took to Jack right away, partly, he said, because he was as dull as they come, which her father took as a sure sign of trustworthiness. Jack's wife, Rhinetta, was director of the Corinth County Home Extension Office, a title Mira had never bothered to have defined but that always reminded her in some crude way of the four major food groups. Their daughter, Samantha, happened to be Kat's age, so everyone but Samantha and Kat figured a friendship between the two was a given, but they had shown no interest in seeing each other outside of school. When her parents pressed her on why, Kat had said they belonged to different groups—that Samantha was popular, that a dozen page numbers followed her name in the yearbook's index, as compared to Kat's one, the truest measure of popularity, she had said to blank stares.

A mile from Jack's office, Mira started imagining how the conversation would go. She would stumble to get out what she had come to say, misinterpret some look of his as censure, and end up defensive. She had a knack for that.

Before turning right into Jack's parking lot, she stopped to wait for a young Hispanic woman to clear the sidewalk. Mira was talking out loud, gesturing with her free hand, saying Jack's lines and her own, both in the same shrill, high-strung voice. Then she realized the woman was watching her as she walked, and the mixed look of insult and horror on her face made it clear that she thought Mira was yelling at her, impatient for her to get out of the way.

Mira pulled halfway into the lot, straddling the car over the sidewalk, and half-yelled out her window, in the same desperate voice as before, that the woman had misunderstood. The woman sped up, her bent arms swinging fast like a power walker's, her rope of braided black hair swinging pendulum-like at her lower back. As she rounded the corner, Mira wondered where the woman was going, who was waiting for her, and whether they would hear about this when she got there, about Mira's random act of hostile ugliness, a blemish on the human race. That Mira had meant no harm didn't matter, because the woman would never know otherwise. As far as the woman was concerned, those were slurs Mira had blurted out, and Mira pulled up next to Jack's Continental feeling as guilty as if they had been.

Jack had just relocated his office to what had been a veterinary clinic—a bland, smallish building of spotty brown and beige brick. Inside, the odor was unmistakable, a mixture of sprays, dips, and flea shampoos. The air smelled toxic.

No one was at the front desk, so she walked down a hallway dotted with futile disk-shaped air fresheners. She found Jack behind his desk in a cordovan chair that seemed to swallow him up like a leather throne. He was emptying his lunch from a padded insulated lunch box.

"Hey, Miss Mira." He said it as if he was surprised to see her. She took a seat across from him. He was in his forties and good-looking in an overly groomed, small-eyed kind of way. His thin hair was combed abruptly away from his left-side part and sprayed into a blade-thin wedge over his forehead, as if an awning there to provide shade.

He held up a Ziploc bag of grapes, asking with his eyebrows if Mira wanted any. She shook her head no. "Rhinetta's into a good lunch," he said.

"How's things?"

"Better yet, how are you? How's Kat?"

"She's better than any of us."

"Yeah, sometimes it's easier for kids to spring back," he said. "They're more elastic that way."

Mira paused, trying to think of just how to phrase things, but Jack couldn't take the silence, started mumbling about the lingering dog hair, then the low-sodium diet Rhinetta was threatening to put the family on. So Mira just blurted out what she had come to ask him.

"How bound am I by the will?" she asked. "To accept what it leaves me?"

"The money?"

"I was thinking of the house."

"You don't want the house?" he asked.

"The moving part. I'm not sure it's the best thing."

"The will's got a special instruction for you to do so." Jack was eating skinny Fritos. Each one looked like a *Guinness Book of World*

Records fingernail. "But as the executor, I'm the one who'd have to force it on you, and I'm not about to do that."

Mira's eyes were focused on his hands, which were small and looked freshly scrubbed and lotioned. His fingers were thin and white, his nails pink and clipped short. No scars, no callus on his middle right finger, no history of nail biting. He had the sheltered hands of a doctor.

"Be painful, I'm sure," he was saying. "There's no time stipulation. Maybe if you give it a year."

"It's not so simple."

"Never is, is it?" Jack responded, somehow a little too quickly. He leaned back in his mammoth chair, denting his diet Coke can, then popping the dents back out.

On the way out, Mira said, "If you should talk to Kearney or Kat, could you leave this out?"

Jack nodded. "Keep me posted."

Two days later, Mira was in Wesley's walk-in closet with a flashlight, the only other light coming from a lamp in the bedroom. A week ago, she had gotten careless, pulled the thin rope that served as the on off switch, then let it snap out of her fingers. It had wound itself around the exposed bulb. The light stayed on for three days before quivering out.

As if she had to keep the pretense up for her own sake, she told herself she was there to scan her father's clothes. He had said they should take what they wanted and give the rest to charity, but for God's sake to make sure it was in a different town. He didn't want sightings of his cardigans and Sansabelts in Mims after he was gone.

Mira found what she had gone in for. The stack of framed pictures was leaning against the back wall of the closet, where she thought she had seen it days earlier. She spotlighted one of them, a painting twenty-four by thirty-six inches, the only work of art her father had ever commissioned. She took it to the bed and centered it on her lap. It was of Lila in 1978, the year before they left.

Helen had trashed any photographs of the house she could get her hands on when Kat was born. Mira had caught her mother in a kitchen chair with a garbage can between her legs, cutting two pictures at a time into squares the size of postage stamps. To let Ona Island linger, she had argued, would be to stir things up needlessly. Mira knew her mother's protectiveness was meant to preserve Kat's affection for her, an affection that was clear to all of them, sometimes uncomfortably so to her father. Whatever the reason, the extreme measures that Helen had forced on all of them to shield Kat from the affair had created in Mira something just short of jealousy. Intense curiosity, maybe.

It was only after Helen died that Wesley decided to have the painting done, though he had never gone so far as to hang it up. For a reason Mira never figured out, Wesley had asked her to go with him to meet the artist, a local oil painter known only as Eve—a tiny, strange woman in her forties who wore shorts with hose and cowboy boots the day they met her. He gave Eve a photograph he had stashed away of the four of them on the front porch, Wesley and Helen standing, Kearney and Mira perched knees to chin at their feet. Wesley's arm was draped around Helen, his hand cupping her shoulder. His other arm hung downward, his hand lightly gripped around the back of Kearney's neck. Helen's hand reached down, her fingers curled under Mira's chin, as if they cradled something valuable, worthy of display, like a Fabergé egg, or an extinct insect.

The photo was the best in a roll taken for the church directory by Aunt Blanche, her father's large, pink-faced sister, whom Helen always described as lowbrow and whose favorite exclamation was "My stars!" But it was Helen who had engineered every detail of the pose: the serene smiles on their faces, the way they were all connected by hands and shoulders and chins, as if part of the same body, overgrown and out of control. They looked like puppets.

Behind them, the house's horizontal wood planks were painted the color of egg yolk. The A-framed tile roof ascended into the trees and powder blue sky at a thirty-degree angle, enough slope to provide for a small attic, accessed by a disappearing stair in the hallway. The attic's only window, perfectly round and made of obscure glass, rested just under the roof's apex. Directly under the eave, a row of dentils—square blocks a couple of inches across—stretched the length of the house's face like teeth. A triangle of fish scale–like imbricated tiles, mustard-colored for contrast, extended down from the dentils. On the left side was a small porch, just big enough for a couple of rocking chairs, and on the right, a picture window the size of a mattress laid sideways.

The house was much longer than it was wide, like a shotgun house, their mother once complained. To this, Wesley had said, "Our ancestors broke their backs to afford shotgun houses, so that should do us just fine." Mira remembered wondering where he had gotten this, what ancestors he was talking about exactly. But maybe she had just followed the lead of Helen, who had reminded him of the long line of pharmacists she came from, then started in on how the house was too quirky, too full of itself—"Look at me, I'm not like any other house," she had said in the lowest voice she could manage—and that it wouldn't have any resale value. To this, her father had responded in his calm way that resale value would never be an issue.

The photo had been taken in the summer, so Eve's painting showed the house in a cloud of green, as if sprouting from the flora itself. A huge pine stood just left of center. Midway up its trunk, two large branches had curved and tangled over decades, creating the look of folded arms, as if the main trunk were the torso, the roots were the legs submerged in the earth, and the needles and pinecones made up the sticky head.

At Wesley's request, Eve had written "Lila" in the painting's foreground in her best cursive, loopy and slanted to the right. She had thought this an odd caption. "Care to explain?" Eve had asked, clawing at a splotch of dried paint on her cheek.

Mira remembered saying something like "Same way people name their boats" and enjoying the look of approval her father sent her. Before they left, he took his chance to ask Eve if she knew anything about death masks. He had seen a picture of Napoléon's once and wondered if the practice was still around. They were both surprised—just short of frightened—when Eve said, "Indeed. Fact is, I just got a commission for one from a Tennessee family."

Now, edged in the crevice between the painting of Lila and its frame were two photos, one of the house under construction, a skeleton of beams, rafters, and studs, foil-lined rolls of roofing paper and blanket insulation waiting to be installed, but for now strewn across the bald yard. Wesley struck a supervisory pose in the foreground.

He had taken the other photo, a fuzzy black-and-white shot, with a camera he had made himself using aluminum foil and other stuff Mira couldn't remember. None of them were in the picture, just the house, looking idle, stagnant. The only sign of life was Wesley's elongated shadow, like a stilt walker's, slanting across the bottom of the photo like some fragment of a person eking his way into the frame, determined to be seen.

Fifteen minutes later, Mira was making random calls to house movers. One company, Movers and Schaeffers, Ltd., said it moved only single and double-wides. Another said it was busy waging a lawsuit over asbestos exposure. Another wasn't certified to move houses interstate. "Only in the Land of Opportunity, ma'am," the owner said in a shrill voice.

Then Mira called Gaar Enterprises, whose creed, according to the Yellow Pages, was "Gaar moves near or far." A perky receptionist put her through to Wayne Gaar, esteemed head of contracts, she said.

In a minute, a voice textured by years of smoke and drink asked, "What can we do for you 'smornin'?"

Not knowing what information he needed, Mira yapped about the details of the move, the size of the house, its age. As she spoke, he cleared his throat several times.

"And is the house currently furnished, ma'am?" She heard a quick sucking noise, as if he was pulling a cigarette away from his lips.

"Just barely. It hasn't been lived in for any length of time in years."

"Childhood home?" he asked, as if this was nothing new to him.

"On and off."

They went back and forth like this for a few minutes. He said it sounded like a job he could take, but he would have to check with the county on the North Carolina end to see about a permit, then contact the Department of Transportation to check on clearances for the route. The house would have to be inspected to make sure it met codes in both states. "All that could take up to two weeks," he told her. "Miss, what was that name?"

"Mira DeLand."

"Okay, Miss Land, judging from your description, it sounds like we could keep her in one piece." He said it slowly, as if in mid-thought or calculation.

"What kind of time frame would we be looking at?" It seemed to Mira like the question to ask, though she had no time constraints, save a general desire to carry this out as soon as possible.

"Well, I've got a team out now that's havin' a hell of a time gettin' this antiquer moved. Mother Goose just passed on, and the ducklings—I guess there are six or seven of 'em—own two plots of land and they're split over which one to move it to." He paused to exhale a mouthful of smoke. "Talked to Ray—that's my son— last evening and he tells me they had the thing within two miles of one site when one of the no-accounts jumped ship and sided with the others."

"Sounds complicated."

"It's a damn pain in my butt's what it is." She heard him flipping through pages. "I'd say if everything's cleared, we can get you set up for mid-June."

"Just in time for the summer heat," she said for the sake of it.

"You and me both." He went on to explain that if his company took the job, he would send a flatbed and two pilot trucks rather than subcontracting, because either way, Gaar Enterprises would be responsible for both legs. A "brother company" in the Ona Island area would be hired to help out on that end. Wayne Gaar didn't explain what that would entail. "And you or someone on your behalf'll have to meet us on the other end. Company policy."

"Understood."

"Movin' a house's not like deliverin' a baby, where you can read the manual and every one's pretty much the same. You could move a hundred houses, start on the hundred and first, and get stumped as to how a house made of ten thousand Arkansas stones—no two the same size and shape—is gonna be divided in half for the move. Tell you the truth, that's what I like about this business."

Wayne Gaar won Mira over with this testimonial of his, partly because she didn't think that was his aim, but just a nice accident of his weathered crankiness.

Sometimes it seemed to Mira as if her father's funeral had been someone else's, as if he'd just stepped out and would be back soon rustling a bag from Sears, or Radio Shack. Reminders of him lingered, like afterthoughts. The leftovers of his cancer: the wheelchair, hospital bed, half-used prescriptions. In his bathroom sink, the ring of shaving dust so fine, he couldn't have seen it to wipe away. The powdered Gatorade he had bought by the case. The trace of Old Spice on his clothes. The dozens of ink-stained rubber bands on the bathroom doorknob from the morning paper. His truck parked in the driveway as he had left it, backed in, as always. Mira missed the sound of him, his falsetto laugh, the squeak of his chair's wheels sunk into the shag, the skim of his hands along his armrests, or his thighs.

And then there were the phone calls. The newspaper had run a prominent obituary, so word spread quickly in town. But calls came from Wesley's clients, an old high school friend arranging a reunion, long-distance phone companies offering the lure of a signing bonus, the bailed-out counterfeiter saying he had a buddy who could run some tests on the livre note. When Mira picked up, she would break the news in as direct terms as possible, but Kat refused to do so. "He's out of town," she would say, or "He can't come to the phone. Can I take a message?" And then she would scribble a name and number on a notepad, as if Wesley were going to step in any second and take care of neglected business. A pointless stack of these lay by the phone. When Mira pressed her on why, Kat came back with "The library's stained-glass window was commissioned by the family to duplicate the exact pattern in the room's woven wool rug," gliding her hand to one side like a game-show hostess. In lieu of the silent treatment, she had recently developed the habit of spouting off lines from her script at Mims's birthplace. And she knew what she was doing. It was maddening.

Three days later, when Wayne Gaar called back and said that he had gotten early clearance for the move, Kat immediately started back in on whether she could make the drive to North Carolina with Mira.

"When am I gonna see Ona Island if I don't see it now?" she whined. Mira was on hold with the utilities company, trying to change the billing name.

"See what?" Mira used her shoulder to hold the phone to her ear. "It makes Mims look like a metropolis."

Kat swiped her flattened hand in front of Mira's face, as if wiping fog from a window. "News bulletin: I wouldn't be going for the museums."

"Don't tell me you don't want to stay with the Scangas for a week."

"I'd rather poke my eyes out with hot needles."

"You're cranky."

"It must be time for my nap."

"Kearney said you could stay with him." Then the operator came back on, and Kat walked out of the room, her head turned toward Mira so she could get a good view of the scowl on her face. A few minutes later, off the phone, Mira found her in the kitchen. She was tearing American cheese slices into quarters, arranging them on saltines.

"Want to drive me to the P.O.?" Mira asked.

"The grandfather clock in the foyer was made specifically for the home." She spoke as succinctly as she could manage, sticking the plate in the microwave. "Its exterior is cedar, salvaged from the home's original foundation, which was severely damaged in the '46 tornado."

This went on for a couple of days. At a loss, Mira just kept rephrasing the same excuse. Then, while she was still dwelling on how to dislodge Kat from her rut, Kat dislodged Mira from hers. Mira was washing dishes when Kat came into the kitchen and started toweling off a colander.

"So you haven't given me any actual reasons why I shouldn't go."

Mira handed her a cheese grater. "Act your age."

"Excuse? I'm acting more your age than you are."

"That's what I mean."

"Whatever." Kat shot Mira her best look of condescension. "Reasons?"

Mira was sure that Kat didn't know what a tough spot this put her in, tough because the only actual reason was the one Kat couldn't know. But for certain, not letting her go would do more to spark her curiosity than anything. That much was easy to figure out.

Mira flicked Kat with suds. "Don't blame me when it's a let-down."

"I'll give notice at work." Kat hugged her from behind, then jogged out of the room.

A minute later, Mira heard Kat on the phone with Kearney, telling him the news. Mira wasn't surprised when he asked to talk to her.

"What's in your head?" he half-yelled. Kat stayed in the room, flipping channels on the muted TV.

"It'll be great, huh?" Mira responded into the phone.

"Kat can't go," he said, quieter now.

"Yeah, and she can see the Smoky Mountains."

"He was clear about what he wanted."

"And Blowing Rock, or Slippery Rock, or whatever that place—"

"What if you see someone you knew, or whom Mom knew?"

"We'll take the camera," Mira said.

"You're stuck with what happens if you take her there."

Kat paused on ESPN and started doing calisthenics along with a tall, ponytailed man on a beach.

"I'll get doubles," Mira promised before hanging up.

Despite his disapproval, Kearney called Mira at eleven two nights later and asked if Kat was in bed yet. When Mira said no, he told her to lie and tell Kat he needed a jump start.

"Just meet me at the bus stop," he urged into his cell phone. He made a left turn, holding the wheel with only his middle finger. It was misting, and his windshield wipers whined.

Mira said she was on her way. As Kearney ran a yellow, he passed the Dairy Queen and remembered the recurring nightmares he had had as a kid involving grain silos and how afterward his father would drive him for a soft-serve if the nightmare came before midnight. This had gone on for months, until his mother accused him of faking to get his dairy fix.

Kearney parked next to the covered shed that the Jaycees provided for bused schoolkids, just a few blocks from the duplex. The rain was heavier now, but he didn't bother with the umbrella as he walked to the bench to wait for Mira. She drove up, and when she sat down next to him, he picked up the smell of the house, not good or bad, just utterly familiar.

"Kat up to no good staying up late?" Kearney grazed a thumb across his shadow of a mustache.

"She's watching Bob Ross," Mira said.

Kearney remembered the art set he had given Kat, with sketchbook, oil paints, and watercolor pencils. Their sister had a knack for rendering, but not much imagination to flesh it out with, she always said, which is one reason she was convinced of her calling as a courtroom sketch artist.

Mira inflated her cheeks. "What's on our agenda?"

"I found this in Dad's files." Kearney handed Mira an envelope made out to Helen in small, jerky handwriting he had recognized as his father's. Inside was a newspaper clipping stapled to a sheet of Wesley's letterhead. Both had tiny creases all over them, like they had been crumpled up. The clipping was from the *Ona Island Ledger,* dated October 1, 1985—an obituary for the Reverend Joseph Bleecher, "respected citizen and minister at Success Baptist Church for three decades." His wife had been gone for twenty years, but he was survived by two kids, grandkids, and others. The letter read:

Love,

Here's some news from Ona Island. Change anything? How about moving Lila? She awaits.

Devotedly yours,

Wes

Kearney lay back on the bench and felt the damp planks through his shirt. He propped a leg on Mira's lap, then joined her in staring at the blur of night rain. He tried to guess at the scene as his mother found the note, whether his father had left it strategically propped up by a napkin holder, or a bottle of White Shoulders. Whether her hair been sprayed into her favorite cascade of Twinkie-size curls, or neglected and windblown, the way it always looked best, the way she hated it. Whether his father had been lurking a room away, listening for signs, or deliberately out of range, maybe talking fertilizer with Ru in the front yard. Whether she had crumpled the note up herself, or saved that for her husband after he had gotten the answer. Kearney knew he couldn't be sure of anything, except that it had been autumn, so his mother would have been in her favorite cardigan, the color of the roux he had seen her make a hundred times. She had always worn the sweater in a way that made her look more frail than she was, just draped over her shoulders, as if she wanted to be ready to commit to sleeves or toss it altogether with the slightest change in temperature.

———

A week before Mira was to make the drive to Ona Island to meet the movers, she got a call from a man who introduced himself as Ray Gaar, the son of Wayne Gaar. He spoke like a tennis commentator, calmly and with little commotion. He was calling to tell her of a glitch in the move.

"One of our team drivers got a better offer and decided it was worth his while to take it," he said. "Harried things up around here."

"What's the prognosis?" she asked.

"We were wondering if you or an adult member of your family might like to drive one of our escort pilot trucks, since one of you has to tag along anyway. It'd get you a twenty percent discount on the rate."

"Anybody can be an escort?"

"How's your driving record?" Ray Gaar said.

"Clean."

"That's all our insurers ask for."

Mira enjoyed the distraction of a week's preparations for the trip, preparations she made as her father would have done, with lists and safeguards and precautions. She canceled her appointment for an oil change, then promised the service manager that she would reschedule when she got back. At first, she didn't bother stopping the newspaper, then she pictured them piling up at the end of the driveway—a sign saying no one's home—and opted to put a hold on it after all. The night before they left, she unplugged the oldest of the lamps, for fear of a short. She scanned the refrigerator for perishables, started to toss out the lactose-free milk and cheese, then decided Kearney might be able to use them.

The morning of the trip, she turned off the air conditioner, then palmed each of the stove burners, just to be sure. When Kearney pulled up to give them a ride, Mira did a final scan of the house. Her eyes landed on the dining room. The flowers had kept coming, ending up on the wooden dining room table, until it looked like a coffin. Knowing they would go to waste otherwise, Mira ran two bouquets over to Ru Biddolf next door. Grateful and bleary-eyed, he was saying something, but it was lost on Mira, suddenly deaf to everything but the hum of Gro-Lites on his African violets. She felt stuck in a montage, things happening so fleetingly that they only need to be set to music and acted out in summary. She wondered if, in the rush, she was about to mouth the wrong line, or take a turn that wasn't intended, risking an end that wouldn't make sense.

 $\mathcal{F}ive$

Over day-old doughnuts, Kat used the twenty-minute drive to Perk, where Gaar Enterprises was based, to convince Kearney and Mira of the evils of computer-simulated age progressions. They were all in the front seat of Kearney's kiwi green Dodge K car.

"They're the spinning jenny of age simulation." Kat used her finger to scoop excess jelly filling back into the box. "The computer programs spit the things out so efficiently that the sketch artists can't compete. They end up doing kiddie caricatures at the county fair Four-H booth."

"No more sugar for you." Mira took the box from Kat's lap and realigned the leftover doughnuts.

"I don't see you looming your own clothes," Kearney said to Kat.

"I shop at Goodwill. I never pay retail."

"I bet it's killing Wal-Mart."

Kat picked a pink sprinkle from Kearney's chin and put it in her mouth. "I still love you, dorkus."

Wayne Gaar's office building was corrugated metal on three sides, but its front was finished off with brick, shutters, brass fixtures, and so on. Four columns supported the roof where it extended five feet in front of the building, covering a concrete slab porch. The thing reminded Mira of an apartment complex she had lived in her senior year in college. An elaborate stucco sign at the entrance had read, THE MANOR AT VERSAILLES, but the only payoff had been a square mile of decrepit apartment buildings, eight units each, soiled mattresses leaning against Dumpsters, foil-covered windows, and four-by-six balconies used for storage.

Wayne Gaar was completely bald. The skin at the base of his neck lay in folds, like a rolltop desk, his skull knobby in places. He had the look of an ex-lineman, a short but wide neck, meaty arms that wouldn't quite lie flat against his sides. Below his hand-hemmed Dickies shorts, his legs bowed and his knees looked patched up with putty. Raised scars cut across them at all angles.

"Ready to truck?" He shimmied a giant invisible steering wheel at ten and two.

Mira grinned and reached to shake his hand. "Nice to meet you."

Ray Gaar, whom Mira had only spoken with on the phone, came out of the French doors at the front of the building. He had the height of his father, without the stomach. They shared the same walk, finished each step high on the ball of their foot, on tiptoe for a fraction of a second.

Ray stepped into the circle they had formed. He stood with a hand on his hip, his thumb and index finger resting on his belt, the other fingers curving downward. A leather knife case was hooked onto his belt loop, and Mira wondered what it would be like to live a life that required a knife to be handy at all times. Ray rested all his weight on one leg, the other pointing slightly forward, as if an ornament, there just to be admired.

"Mira DeLand, I take it."

"Ray Gaar, I take it." They shook hands. His eyes matched his denim shirt, which looked as if it had been through years of washes. "This is Kearney." Mira waved her hand to the left.

And before Mira could do so, Kat introduced herself. "I'm Sister Kat." When Ray reached his hand out, she held hers up to his face, her wrist cocked. This bit caught him off guard—he flashed his eyes to the ground and laughed in his throat—but he kissed her hand anyway.

Wayne smiled and palmed his round stomach like a pregnant woman. "If that's not sweet."

A twentyish guy had just driven up in the kind of low-riding accessorized truck that Mira associated with hand car washes. He parked in the only shady spot in the mostly empty lot. PICKIN AND GRINNIN was airbrushed on his truck's tailgate.

"This one's gonna be the third in this trio." Then Wayne volunteered that Aron was a councilman's son who had failed to make the grades to keep a swimming scholarship a few years ago, dropped out, and been moving houses ever since. Aron caught the last bit of this as he walked up, and he thanked Wayne for the introduction as he wiped his palm on his jeans, then shook everyone's hand. He held a duffel bag over one shoulder, a camera by a strap over the other.

"You should get in there tomorrow night." Wayne was pinching an unfiltered cigarette between his thumb and forefinger, his other three fingers curled into his palm. When he put the thing to his mouth and let go, squinting as he inhaled, his fingers stayed in the same position, poised to take the cigarette back out when the time came. "The move'll take a couple days. Drive back should go slower."

"Won't average but about thirty-five," Aron said.

Wayne went on: "Ray and I'll be in touch along the way."

Kearney asked if anyone wanted the rest of the doughnuts for the trip. Kat and Mira declined, but Aron grinned widely and reached out a hand. Then Kearney told them to keep him posted.

"We've got your cell number," Mira said.

He kissed them both on the cheek. "Check your blind spots." The smile he wore for Kat's benefit faded a little as he looked at Mira.

Ray's truck was an eighteen-wheeler with a flatbed. The cab was bright red, with Gaar's company name and address on each door. The escort trucks were small white pickups, what they had called "sissy trucks" as kids. Orange flags pointed out of each end of the windshield like antennae, with two rectangular lights in between. Ray followed Mira and Kat to their pickup.

"Here's a map with our route highlighted and a rundown of the roads we'll take, just in case," he said, "though I s'pose you've been this way before." As he handed Mira the keys, she stole a look at his wedding band, a braid of three clusters of wire-thin gold strands.

"Am I front or back?" Mira asked.

"Rear both legs," Ray said. "Aron'll take the front. We're all linked by CBs, got a range of a few miles, so no worries if we get separated."

Mira's eyes were on Ray's light brown hair, which was receding, and she decided this made him look older than she, though nothing else about him hinted at that. She had once told a man she was dating that she found receding hairlines attractive. He had one of his own and took her compliment as sympathy. Now, she wondered if Ray worried about losing his own hair when he looked at his father's glossy scalp.

Ray reached across her lap and turned on the CB. "This is a

mobile rig. It's got forty channels, but you can leave it where it is, on nineteen." He held the microphone a couple of inches from his mouth. "No need to choke yourself with it. Press the lever down to speak. Breaker one-nine, this is Big Rig for a demo. Over."

Within a few seconds Aron's voice rattled back, "This is Walker Talker. You're loud and clear. Over."

"Ten-four." Then to Kat and Mira, Ray said, "That means, I got your transmission and agree with it."

"What does CB stand for?" Mira wondered aloud.

Ray placed the microphone back on its notch and started to answer, but Kat beat him to it.

"Citizens band."

"Where'd you pick that up?" Mira asked.

"Nickelodeon." Kat batted her eyes for effect, twitching her bangs, which hung low and webbed with her lashes.

Ray walked back toward his rig, and when halfway there, he turned around and yelled back their way, "Handles, my dears."

Ray's smell lingered after he left. It was Old Spice, unmistakable, as familiar to Kat as the color of her father's eyes, or the shape of his hands. He had never strayed from his morning routine, and as a child, she had always caught the end of it while she watched *Captain Kangaroo* reruns on his bed after breakfast but before school. He would put on his work pants, zip and button them, slide on his belt, feeling for the belt loops without looking away from the TV, and fasten the buckle. Then he would sit on the corner of the bed and slide a fist into each sock to loosen it before putting it on. He would save his shirt for last, which always struck her as odd, because once it was on, he would have to go back and undo his belt and pants to tuck his shirt in. After all this, he would slather himself in Old Spice, douse it on his palm, which he would swipe behind his neck, then another douse and a swipe through his still-damp hair.

Kat looked over at Mira and knew from the glassiness of her eyes, which were aimed at her, that she had smelled it, too.

Mira's first road trip behind the wheel had been at sixteen. Her mother had forced her to drive nonstop three hundred miles by herself in the brown Fury after she had taken the car to an off-limits party instead of a baby-sitting job she had trumped up. Her mother called the house where Mira said she would be (allegedly to see that everything was okay) and the confused mother blew her cover. Mira was later amazed that she had thought her plan to be so flawless.

Helen decided that she should drive ahead of Mira in the Scamp as she carried out her sentence. "Else you might find a dead end and sack out," her mother said.

"You could check the odometer," Mira told her.

To that, she responded, "Pipe down."

So the next morning, Helen sent her husband out to gas up the cars. It was a family rule that the cars had to be gassed up before they left the driveway for a trip, not on the way out of town, never that.

A few hours into the drive, when her mother stopped to refill and get a snack, she motioned for Mira to stay in the Fury. When Mira started to roll down her window, her mother shook her head and moved her forearm in a circle, signaling for Mira to leave it up. Mira waved her over and mouthed that she needed to use the bathroom, but Helen told her to stay put. Mira yelled through the glass that people had died of bladder infections from holding it, that it had happened to some Danish astronomer whose name she couldn't remember. Her mother stuck her face right up next to the window and said, "I'll make you wish you had a bladder infection." The glass in front of her mouth fogged as she spoke, and Mira felt like a dog jerked back to its spike by a fully extended leash.

Her mother had decided on three hundred miles by multiplying by ten the number of illicit miles Mira had driven to the party. "You'll get swallowed up by ten times as much shit when I'm not around to steer you straight," she had warned. This bit of nastiness was harsher than Mira was used to getting, even from her mother, but it worked. Her words taunted Mira as she drove that day, once bringing her to tears, so that she had to flip down the visor and wear sunglasses in hopes that Helen wouldn't see her crying from the Scamp ahead.

Toward the end of the drive, though, Mira felt herself start to enjoy the whole thing. She decided she liked playing the role of martyr. And knowing that martyrs had to have a cause, she decided her cause that day was demonstrating—to whom, she wasn't sure—her mother's indefatigable need to have the family under her thumb, and their own masochistic willingness to help her carry that out.

 *Six*

They were about twenty miles east of Perk. The air had the sweaty feel of a greenhouse, the smell some mixture of runoff and rotting grass from the ditch along the shoulder. The clouds, like a cluster of white islands on a pastel blue sea, threw shadows onto the highway. With no AC, Mira and Kat had the windows rolled down all the way. Kat was drawing in her sketchbook and listening to music in her headphones, whose buzz Mira could just make out over the whip of the wind.

"This's Big Rig." Mira was startled by the static of Ray's voice over the CB. "How's it feel? Over."

She rolled her window up halfway to hear the CB, then fumbled beneath the ashtray for the microphone. "Hi."

"Nice CB speak. Over."

"Are my escort lights supposed to be on?"

"Not till we've picked up the house," Ray answered. "So've you thought of a handle yet? Over." She could hear the throaty hum of the rig's engine in the background.

"What's wrong with Mira?"

"That's not very catchy."

"Where'd Big Rig come from?" Mira asked. Kat yanked her head-phones off by the cord to listen in.

"I'm always the one driving the flatbed."

"Fair enough."

A gleaming late-model pickup passed on their left. The driver—a pencil-thin elderly man wearing a beret—looked Mira's way and lifted a couple of knuckly fingers from the steering wheel in a le-thargic wave, smiling with the same limited energy.

"So yours is my one hundred and eightieth house," Ray said.

"How do you know?"

"I keep a log." He sounded like an astronaut speaking to ground control, grainy and remote.

"Dad would like him," Kat said, almost to herself. She was sketching her left foot, which was bare and resting on the dash-board.

"So are you the only heir?" Mira said into the microphone.

"To the Gaar fortune."

"Fortune, huh?"

"Enough to keep everybody happy, support my mom's arts and crafts addiction." Ray signed off for a minute, then came back, the connection weaker than before. "Hot damn! The next weigh sta-tion's closed. Saves us an hour."

Kat pulled the microphone by its cord until it sprung free from Mira's hand. "So what about your wife?" Kat asked.

Mira did an Elvis curl of her upper lip and frowned a neat row of creases into her forehead.

"My life?"

"Wife," Kat said a little louder.

"What about her?" Ray asked, as if bored with the question.

"Just—what's she like?" Mira used one of Kat's drawing pencils to fake-gag herself.

"We're separated," Ray said. Kat widened her eyes toward Mira. "Her name's Liz."

"I used to want to be named that."

"She sells garage doors. Lives for it. Commercial, residential, sectional, one-piece steel, insulated, wood-paneled. You name it."

"Sounds like the garage door guru."

"She'd take that as a compliment."

It had begun to rain. A warm mist of it blew in the window. The smell was a mixture of bitter rain and recently laid asphalt. In an instant, it became a downpour, the thick drops rattling percussion-like against the truck's roof.

"Watch these roads," Ray said. "Over and out."

Kat cradled the microphone, then held her pad out the window for just a second, letting the rain dampen her sketched foot. She skimmed her finger over its toes and arch, blurring the edges.

In midmorning, they crossed the Mississippi. The spring had set records for its lack of rainfall, so the river was low, exposing about ten feet of the riverbed. Throwaway tires and the roots of extinct trees jutted out, half-entombed in the cinnamon-colored dirt. As they crossed the state line, Kat wedged her hand as far forward as it would go where the windshield met the dashboard. "Beat you to Tennessee," she announced. The other variation of this game they had played as kids was to see who could be the first to breathe a state's air. The trick was waiting until just the right moment to crack your window.

The first stop was at a Loaf-N-Jug. A spray of cool air met them on the way in. Behind the counter, a smallish clerk with RORY embroidered on his shirt pocket was loading packs of cigarettes into a dispenser. As if he had done it a thousand times, he exhaled a melodic "How y'all?" An attractive, though emaciated, woman sat just behind him in a lawn chair, working a crossword puzzle in a book of them. Her hair, dyed the color of merlot, seemed twice the size of her head.

The only bathroom's lock was broken, so Kat and Mira guarded the door for each other. The place smelled of urine and cherry concentrate. The floor was clammy and littered with beds of soggy toilet paper. The roll on the dispenser was puckered, as if it had gotten damp, then dried, and a revolving cloth hand towel looked suspiciously like it had gone around more than once without being laundered.

Kat squatted over the toilet. "Nothing beats peeing in a life-size petri dish." They managed to leave without touching a single surface—flushed with their shoes and palmed wads of toilet paper for the faucet and door handle.

When they came out, Mira found Ray in the medicine section of the miscellaneous aisle, where he was scanning the travel packs of antacids, antihistamines, laxatives. "I love these." He fingered a package of aspirin, two doses. "They're so personalized."

"They've got a way of charging extra for that oozing goodness you feel."

He sighed in mock exasperation, locking his eyes on hers as he took a sip of his chocolate drink, waiting for her mock apology in return.

Mira flashed him a smile. "Sorry."

At the register, Rory rang up the gas, drinks, and Kat's Nerds, which looked like discarded candy crumbs. "Where's this convoy headed?" Rory asked. His hair was thinning severely, though he had tried to make the most of the few patches he had, combing them in alternating directions and dying them a dark brown that had left his scalp a shade darker than the surrounding skin.

"Ona Island, North Carolina," Ray answered.

Rory's eyes widened. "I've gotta couple of exes near there. Think they've formed a club against me. They call it Damn Rory to Hell."

Ray got a kick out of this. "Card-carrying members, huh?"

"You know it." Rory laughed and swiveled his head to look at the woman behind him. Pointing at her with his thumb, he said, "My fiancée." He pronounced it like *finance* without the first *n*. "Here's your slipper dipper." He handed Ray the receipt. "You kids stop back by on your second leg."

Back on the interstate, the rain had stopped. Pillows of steam rose from the road as if from a fresh stretch of tar.

"Roadkill ahead." It was Aron. The CB served his voice well, filtered out some unpleasant sharpness Mira couldn't put her finger on. Not bothering to reach for the microphone, she kept her eyes open for the dead animal. It was flattened beyond identity, like a slightly raised brown and red mole on the highway.

After a few minutes, Ray came in over the CB. "So when's the last time you made this drive?"

The question threw Mira. As clearly as anything, she could picture things as they had been: the clammy August air, the new tightness of her Gloria Vanderbilt jeans around her waist, the only tape she had had for the drive, a demo of ballads and medleys that had come with the Fury. It felt so recent, the answer surprised her.

"Eleven years ago."

"You were a young thing," Ray said.

Mira looked over at Kat. She had fallen asleep, her legs curled up on the seat, head cocked at an angle against the locked door. She had never heard the story, had been too young to keep track of time when she was told Mira was visiting family for a month.

"I was seventeen. My mother sent me to the old house to have a baby." Kat opened her eyes and adjusted them toward Mira, who could tell from the look on Kat's face that she had heard as clearly as anything.

There was no immediate comeback from Ray, and Mira imagined him lowering the microphone to his lap, then making a hundred instant adjustments to his first impression of her, and she wondered what that had been, what she had blown. She drove over a dip in the road. The microphone brushed against her lips.

Mira looked at Kat. "Where'd you think I got all those stretch marks?" Mira knew immediately that it had come out sounding more flip than she wanted it to.

Kat rotated her legs onto the floor, adjusting the tightness of her seat belt. "Who was the father?"

"My debate partner, Chad Broussard," Mira said, her thumb back on the CB button. "He had this charming nerdiness. It charmed me, anyway. At the end of every rebuttal speech, he'd say, 'I ask for your acquiescence.' What could be sweeter?"

Ray answered this. "My first kiss was in the fourth grade with my bus driver's . . ." There was a whistling noise and his voice faded out, then faded back in just as quickly. ". . . A year ahead of me. She got called Heidi 'Knickers' Vickers because she wore home-sewn culottes every damn day."

"Okay, you win." Mira cracked her window and heard the flag

just outside whipping in the wind. They passed a sign that warned of construction a mile ahead.

"I'm gonna see if I can get anything on this," Ray said, then added, "Over and out," which he got out in two syllables. Mira slid the microphone back onto the notch.

"So I confided in Dad, who held out for a long weekend before telling Mom."

"That was lovely."

"I pouted for a couple days, but now my theory is that I actually wanted him to tell her, like I figured I deserved whatever she did, which was not to let me tell Chad about the baby. Since it was late summer, she kept me out my senior year, sent me on the drive to Ona Island by myself. When I got there, Aunt Blanche was sitting on the front porch in this purple rocking chair. She had a skirt full of pecans and was edging them one at a time between the rocker and the porch, cracking them that way."

"It was a glandular thing," Kat said with a roll of her eyes. It had become a bit of a joke that each time Aunt Blanche's name was mentioned, her near-disabling heft was shrugged off as a glandular problem, though no one seemed to know or ever ask what that meant exactly. She had died of heart disease in her fifties.

"So Aunt Blanche came at me with one of her hugs and goes, 'My stars, have the tears fallen in torrents on this family.' She got me settled. Mom had the power and water turned on but said no to a phone, said she wouldn't pay for it until the ninth month, so Dad had it hooked up himself without telling her, just had the bill sent to his office."

"But you had a car," Kat said.

"Aunt Blanche impounded it first thing. I never left the house. Mom said she'd see to it that my felt needs were met. Aunt Blanche was an R.N. and a midwife, so they figured it was all within the bounds of legality. Every night, she'd bring me a plate of whatever she'd fixed at home, some loaf thing, usually: meat loaf, ham loaf, olive loaf. She'd always sit with me while I ate it, then take the plate back with her."

Mira veered left to avoid a piece of tire tread arcing upward like a huge rubber claw.

"So I had six months to think of names. I was going with Grace Gretchen for a girl, Wesley Chad for a boy."

"Six?"

"She was stillborn," Mira said. "The umbilical cord had wrapped three times around her neck."

Kat's eyes widened to near circles, as if the possibility that the baby had died hadn't occurred to her; she had assumed adoption.

Mira went on: "Being there, it was like how the ancient Athenians used to banish a different person every year, you know?"

"Nope. I fail the cool test," Kat mumbled.

"That's where the word *ostracism* comes from—the piece of pottery they'd cast their votes on."

"I'd always wondered about the etymology of that word," Kat said, but the way her voice stayed flat, her eyes glazed, cutting down at an angle toward the floor mat, Mira knew Kat was only half-thinking about what she was saying. She knew how Kat felt, like when you first hear about someone dying, someone you knew from a distance, like your best friend's grandmother, or Natalie Wood. You have to repeat it to yourself, picture the person alive, then dead, as if their dying doesn't become real until you've replayed it in your mind a few times.

The construction turned out to be some minor repairs to a

bridge over what used to be Kickshaw Creek, now a gorgeous bed of out-of-control kudzu.

After a couple of minutes, Mira went on. "So when I got home, Mom treated me like a patient discharged from rehab—you know, like I was ready to do the family right, almost like she was congratulating me."

"Where was I?" Kat asked.

"Right there," Mira said. "You gave me a drawing you'd done of me while I was gone. You were sweet."

Kat's eyes were aimed at the dark green hills in the distance, their trees shrunk to nubs. "She was so protective." Kat said this in a way that made it clear she meant it as praise.

"Of our reputation for moral purity, maybe."

"Of you," she said, as if it was obvious, something that shouldn't have to be said. "Say it'd lived. How would you have finished school?"

"I missed the rest of high school anyway."

"What about a baby with no father?"

"I can attest that there was a father," Mira said. A rusty Camaro passed. Thick plastic had been duct-taped on to replace the missing passenger window. A blur of a person seemed to be looking Mira's way from the other side.

"I mean husband," Kat said.

"She's the one who decided he'd never know."

"She made sure you had a nurse."

"Geriatric nurse, and one who wasn't big on anesthesia."

Kat cringed. "How bad was it," she asked, "on a scale of one to ten?"

"Off the scale." Mira felt for an instant as if she was sensationalizing, then decided otherwise, since what she had said seemed to be true.

Then, as if Mira had given her something else to mull over, Kat settled into a stoic gaze out her window.

Mira rolled hers all the way down. The wind whipped her hair, the ends stinging into her cheeks and neck. The dashes of white dividing the lanes whirred by so fast, they became a solid line, and Mira marveled that what she had allowed Kat to hear, as a dare to herself, maybe as some test of the waters, Kat had taken as further evidence of Helen's infallibility.

The narrow strips of Tennessee interstate slivered through high marbleized cliffs, then clusters of lumpy green hills speckled with signs for Rock City, an occasional clearing for two or three houses, their roofs grooved and rusted, the road leading to them lost in the trees. Some of the houses seemed so decrepit that Mira would decide they were uninhabitable, then see clothes on a line, or an exposed lit bulb on a porch.

As all of this faded to shadow with the setting of the sun, Mira might as well have been back in the house. She remembered becoming numb to the pain, ceasing to notice it after a while, barely noticing until much later that she had never seen the baby that Aunt Blanche urged out of her and discarded like leftovers. Afterward, on the drive home, the numbness had worn off, and Mira swore she could feel Aunt Blanche clutching the backs of her thighs with sweaty, fleshy hands, each squeeze a cue to push.

That night, they checked into the It'll Do Motel somewhere around the two hundredth mile marker in Tennessee. They all had the special—hamburger pizza with sides of macaroni and cheese and

Veg-All—at the 1-40 Diner next door to the motel. Over dinner, they got the spectacle of a man in his sixties, sitting at a table with what looked to be his grandkids, with a toothpick sticking up from behind his bottom teeth. With its tip just inside his right nostril, he pushed his nose upward with careful flexes of his jaw. The children went giddy.

While they were waiting for the check, Aron asked if anyone was up for a swim in the motel pool. "It'll wash the grime off."

To this, Kat said, "Let's don't and say we did."

"I didn't bring my suit," Mira said.

Kat tossed a balled napkin into her ice glass. "Me, either."

"It's not a country club. Go in shorts and a T-shirt." When Aron saw that no one was swayed, he added, "I bought an underwater cam." Ray had stayed neutral until then, but the camera was enough to persuade him, so they all ended up going.

The peanut-shaped pool sat just a few car lengths from the road, right next to the office, and smelled a little too much like chlorine. There were no tables, just a few unraveling lounge chairs and a half-deflated pink inner tube. There was no sun left, and the place was poorly lit. A single floodlight under the office's eave mixed with the overflow light from the street. They had the pool to themselves except for a bikini-clad teenager on a lounge chair. She was either asleep or hiding behind sunglasses, and at first glance she reminded Mira of a much younger Crystal Gayle.

Ray hadn't brought a pair of shorts, so he had to go in his jeans, which were already on the tight side. "You're gonna have to cut those off," Kat said, half-submerged, her arms out to her sides. She squealed as she inched into deeper water.

Mira nudged one of her shoes off with the other foot, then stuck a toe in. "It's like ice."

"Are you kidding?" Aron said from the diving board, snapping the waistband of his Speedo. "It's warmer than my bathtub. Fact, this saves me a shower." He bounced for momentum, then did a cannonball. The first clap was followed by a deeper thud as his full weight hit the water.

Ray had taken off his shirt and was in up to his hips, flicking water onto his chest to adjust. His left arm was sunburned from the bicep down.

"That leaves you," Kat said, looking at Mira, who then took off her other shoe and started for the steps. The pool was lit up by underwater lights the size of Frisbees, one on each side. Mira could make out dark spots on the pool's bottom, some stationary, some shifting from the jets. She dodged them as she moved toward the deep end.

Aron climbed up the side ladder and ran on his toes to get the camera from a lounge chair, cursing the cool air as he went. "I knew we'd hit a pool or two." Back in the water, he dipped the disposable camera underwater for a second, then held it up to the dim light, testing for leakage. "Okay, y'all get in line next to that drain. Squat underwater when I say go."

Crystal Gayle raised her sunglasses to her forehead and squinted toward Aron. "It won't come out there," she said. "You don't have a flash." Aron squinted back at her, then took a closer look at the front of the camera.

"Fine, scoot over there." He waved them toward one of the underwater lights. "Ray, you get in the middle." They waddled to where the pool bottom leveled off to four feet. "Now as soon as you get to the bottom, look my way." At Aron's count of three in Spanish, the four of them sucked in as much air as they could and ducked under, Kat and Mira with pinched noses.

When she felt Ray guiding her down, Mira opened her eyes. Ray was already sitting cross-legged on the bottom. Kat was squirming up out of the water, her arms and legs flailing. Already needing air, Mira followed her.

"What was that sorriness?" Aron asked when they were all above water.

Kat tilted her head to each side to drain her ears. "I can't help that I float."

"You're each gonna need to hold one of them down," the girl called out, adjusting her bikini bottom as she stood up. Under her lounge chair was a hard-sided light blue suitcase and a pile of clutter Mira couldn't make out. "Want me to take a group?"

"If it's no trouble," Aron said—borderline shyly, Mira thought.

The girl dove in and swam underwater until she came up a foot from Aron. "No trouble at all." She swiped water from her face.

This time, Mira used Ray as an anchor, gripping his arm as he sank, and Kat did the same with Aron. When Mira felt Ray palming the top of her head, she opened her eyes and looked at the girl. Bubbles perked out of her nose and mouth as she waved her arms upward, trying to keep herself down, her yard-long hair fanning out peacocklike. When she was steadied, she raised the camera to her face and shot.

For the next hour, they took turns staging photos. At Aron's request, Kat and the girl did some synchronized swimming. Mira did the dead man's float. Ray took a picture of Aron standing in front of one of the jets, focusing on the grotesque indentation it made in Aron's stomach. Then Aron asked the girl to take pictures of his butterfly; he figured he could pick out some flaws if he could see his own stroke frame by frame.

It was then that Ray got Mira alone. She had toweled off and was sitting on a lounge chair. Ray walked stiff-legged toward her, his jeans like a wet suit, and took a seat beside her.

"Wayne says he's a fireball." Ray nodded toward Aron.

"He's gonna wear us out before we get home." Mira fingered a piece of her chair's webbing that had come loose. "How come Wayne, not Dad?"

"I can't remember how that started."

Aron had the camera now and was dipping just under the surface to shoot Kat and the girl as they dove into the water.

"So where's your kiddo?" Ray said this like he figured it was with the father or at computer camp.

"She was stillborn." His apology was drowned out by Kat's splash, but Mira looked at him as if to say, Thanks, that it was fine. After a minute, Mira said, "Sorry for Kat's third degree about your wife. Her mouth filter is still being fitted."

"No biggie." His head was cocked back and he was scanning the sky, as if trying to find the Big Dipper, or the moon. "It's a trial is all, just to see how it plays out."

"You must be big on patience." Mira wrung the water from her T-shirt, watching the glittery splash it made against the concrete.

"I love her, so being patient's the easy part. I think she loves me, even though she denies it. I ask her why, and she says she doesn't know, that she just realized it gradually, like how your eyes adjust to the darkness. And anyway, she says she doesn't have to have a reason not to love me. What the hell can you say to that?" Mira could tell Ray didn't expect or want an answer. This seemed like his gentle way of closing the subject.

They stayed at the pool until ten, when the night manager came to lock the gate. Everyone headed toward their rooms, except for Aron and the girl, who ambled in the opposite direction. When

Aron yelled back their way, "I'll drop her off at Wal-Mart's before we hit the road," Mira wondered whether he meant the film or the girl.

That night, her eyes still burning from the chlorine, Mira fell asleep to the leftover sensation of driving the pickup, vibrating and swaying with the pockmarks and curves in the road. Her last woozy thought was of Heidi Vickers and Chad Broussard. They were debating in home-sewn culottes, then asking for the acquiescence of schoolkids whose running footsteps drummed like thunder against the rubberized floor of the Blue Bird school bus.

 Seven

When they pulled up at the IHOP across the street the next morning and found the girl, bags and all, eating pancakes with apple compote under the Moroccan flag, Aron blurted out a quick explanation of how Felissa Scodie was going to tag along for a while and she swore to high heavens she was eighteen.

"Or else sixteen and a runaway." Ray was holding the door open for a guy in rust-colored corduroys scattered with holes, like they had been worn in a shoot-out.

They joined Felissa at an oversized corner booth. "Morning merry sunshines," she said. "Anybody else have total red eye?"

Up close and in daylight, Felissa looked more weathered than she had at the pool. Her hair was the darkest brown, and brittle, as if it had seen too many perms. Her eyes were sweet and made up, but her skin looked like it was recovering from a peel. Just below and to the right of her bottom lip lay a quarter-size scar, the skin there stretched and shiny, as if from a burn. Mira guessed she wasn't much older than Kat.

"Wayne'll be in a four-foot hover," Ray said, looking at Aron.

No one said anything, and Felissa took visual inventory of the looks on their faces, then started in. "Okeydokey, I can see I'm

surrounded by worrywarts, so here's my spiel. You can decide for
yourselves whether I'm a security threat. I don't technically qualify
as a runaway because I'm eighteen, which is not to deny that I am
taking a sabbatical from my parents because it's been brought to
my attention that my father dearest—chief executive asshole of Scodie's Fireworks—is having an affair with his wholesaler, and my
mother tells me she's sticking around anyway. What I wanted to
say to her was, Sure, Mom, they say any shit marriage is worth
fighting for, but instead I decided to hit the road, since they'd just
stopped paying for my cosmetology school tuition anyway, saying
it was a frivolous career path—Not like the fireworks biz, I wanted
to say, but didn't, because I can restrain myself when it's called for.
So currently, I'm taking an educational and parental hiatus, if anyone asks what my status is." Felissa topped off her coffee from the
carafe on the table, then spoke slowly as she wrote in the margin
of her paper place mat, "I, Felissa Scodie, am of legal age and take
full responsibility for my physical and emotional well-being." She
signed and dated it, then slid it toward Ray. "You're free and clear."

Mira flashed her eyebrows at Ray, then looked back to Felissa.
"You've won *me* over."

"*Moi aussi*," Aron said. Not yet aware that Aron's lapses into
other languages came too often, Felissa found this charming. She
was the first person Mira had ever seen who could laugh without
widening her mouth.

Ray lifted his coffee cup to the center of the table. "Cheers, then."
They all clinked and took a first look at their menus.

After breakfast, Ray splayed his *Trucker's Atlas*—the best gift he
had ever received, he said—across the table. He said their ETA was
five o'clock that afternoon if they could match yesterday's pace. It
wasn't as humid as the day before, but brighter, and Mira held her

hand to her forehead in a salute for shade as they headed toward the trucks.

Just about the time they reached interstate speed, a Landlubber model RV passed them, shadowing the pickup. It was glossy beige, with blue and gray contour stripes, pulling a Geo Metro and going seventy. Stuck on the back, just below the GOOD SAM CLUB sticker, was a black outline of the United States, all of the states filled in except in the Northwest. A kid, maybe ten years old, was opening a sliding window in the back. He disappeared, then returned with his hands cupped closed and held out in front of him. He stuck his arms out the window and let go. A parakeet, lemon yellow with green highlights, never had a chance to right its wings and was blown backward, flittering out of sight.

Kat flashed a look at Mira. "Oh my God."

"Did you see that?" Mira asked, knowing she had. Mira glanced at the side mirror. A Cadillac Seville with lobbing curb feelers was about to pass in the left lane.

"Was that real?" Kat pointed a finger in the RV's direction. The kid had moved away from the window, and the RV was too far ahead now for Mira to see the drivers, whether they were in on what had happened.

"Maybe it was being abused," Mira said.

"By the kid's dad or something."

"Or it had a terminal case of mites."

The Cadillac glided up beside them. A row of clothes hung on a rod that extended the length of the backseat. The driver, an elderly man, was talking and gesturing, steering with just a thumb and index finger. A white-haired woman in the passenger seat wore wraparound sunglasses and had her neck in a U-shaped pillow. She was shaking her head slowly, either at the bird or the driver—Mira wasn't sure which.

Kat stared off to the side of the road. "I bet the parents were gonna sell it."

"So the kid figured he'd let it go?"

"If you love something..." Kat pressed her flattened hand against her chest, eyes aimed at the sky.

"Better off than Antoinette," Mira said. She'd been their only parakeet. Kat and Mira had come home to find their mother kneeling in front of the toilet. In her outstretched palm lay Antoinette, drenched and motionless, her beak parted, exposing a tongue no bigger around than a Q-Tip.

"That was the first time I ever saw Mom cry," Kat said.

Mira flashed Kat a look, confused. "She wasn't crying."

"She was so."

"But she wasn't."

"Don't get me irked."

"Okay, maybe she was," Mira lied.

Kat slumped down in the seat, her socked feet wedged between the dashboard and the windshield. "Doesn't seem like three years."

"Time passes more quickly for kids," Mira said. "Kid years are like dog years."

Kat stretched her leg out toward Mira and nudged a toe into her cheek. "Nice parenting skills."

When people asked how her mother had died, Kat's stock answer was that she had had a stroke. But it was more than a little misleading to say she had died of it. Her mother had been home alone when it happened, in the hallway, using the upright vacuum. Kat found her stretched out on her stomach, face flat to the floor, arms extended straight above her head. Her right hand still clasped the handle of the vacuum, which had rolled onto its back but was still running, whining as it sucked in only air. Kat could remember more clearly than she wanted to the smell of the vacuum's overheated motor.

When the ambulance came, her mother was still unconscious. Kat was sure she was dead then, that the paramedics were just trying to protect her when they said over and over, "She's breathing, sweetie."

But she came to within an hour of arriving at the hospital, and within a couple of days, she could manage to get around with a walker. Her speech was garbled, her face partly paralyzed, but she had enough movement in her right hand to write, so she started wearing a notepad and pen on a string around her neck. When the doctor discharged her under the condition that she come in for outpatient physical therapy, she immediately began pushing their father to let her get back into her routine.

More than anything, she wanted to drive. She would write notes in her stilted script, pleading with her husband, as passionately as Kat would three years later, to let her take the car to the grocery store, the bank, anywhere, even if he insisted on being in the car with her, just let her drive. When her husband reasoned that she didn't have the reaction time, she would send him what was intended as a look of disapproval, though after the stroke, it wasn't always easy to tell what expression she was shooting for.

It was a week after she had been released from the hospital that Helen got out of bed in the middle of the night, took Wesley's keys, and headed for the front door without waking anyone.

They all jerked awake to the sound of the car slamming into the brick, clear through to the kitchen. Ru Biddolf had somehow beaten them there. The car's front doors were blocked, so he had climbed in the back and was bent over the seat, patting Helen's shoulder with his skeleton hand, his eyes the size of silver dollars.

The car was still in drive but going nowhere, its front wheels stuck in a crooked spin, propped a foot off the floor by fallen bricks and the crushed kitchen table. Her body drooped sideways in the front seat, her bloody face shining in the motion-detecting lights Wesley had installed just under the house's eave. They found the walker on its side halfway down the front steps. Her knees and palms were scraped where she had fallen and crawled the rest of the way to the car.

That Kat insisted on giving the eulogy hadn't surprised anyone, but no one knew, least of all Kat, whether she could get through it. Wesley had one of his own ready just in case. But Kat made it fine, her voice wiggling just a little when she said she had always been her mother's angel, and now her mother would be hers.

The eulogy done, Kat spent the next three months like a car idling too low, sulking around the house in panties and a T-shirt, saying almost nothing, whispering when she did, eating like a bird, sleeping more than she had thought a person could. The rest of them stayed nearby, watching for change, poised to nurture. Her friends came by, ready to dispense fresh gossip. Samantha Scanga called to see if Kat wanted to go walk the mall. Kat turned them all away, sending one-word refusals through her family.

The Friday before Labor Day, her father came into Kat's room and told her he had put in a call to her school counselor explaining that she needed more time. When she said nothing, he lingered, then told her that grief was like a bruise, the way it festers and you think it will never go away, but one day it does. He left her alone, and in a moment of thirteen-year-old melodrama, she gave her shin an intentional kick against the dresser and waited for the bruise to appear. When it did, she monitored it daily, watching it change shape and color like a mood ring, before it faded away a week later. She remembered deciding then that time was up, grief or no grief.

It was then that she came out of her room after skipping dinner one night, dressed for the first time all day. In the center of the new kitchen table, she placed a stack of forty-nine drawings of her mother, one for every year she had lived. With each one, her features evolved in subtle, almost undetectable ways: eyes deepened, nose grew, skin wilted, bones realigned.

The next day, Kat woke her father up before sunrise and told him that she wanted to go to school. He kissed her chin, then guided her head into the crook between his arm and chest. They had slept there for an hour before waking again to the faraway sound of AM talk radio.

Kat felt as if she had been given a tranquilizer, like some out-of-control primate, to anesthetize, or desensitize, one that eventually would wear off when no harm could be done, when the painful part was over. As quickly as she had dropped out, she stepped back into the thirteen-year-old line of Friday nights loitering at the mall, a fascination with top-forty radio, and crushes on svelte, unattainable boys.

That her grief had been so oddly expressed, that it had even seemed, though no one ever said as much aloud, disproportionate to everyone else's, went as unexplained as the reason for Helen's stroke. Afterward, though, they all accepted it as some inexplicable thing that had been beyond their control, as if labeling it in that way absolved them of the burden of trying to make any sense of it.

Just after hitting the eastern time zone, they stopped for lunch at a place called Trucker's Oasis outside of Knoxville. It had been featured on *America's Truckin'*, the one show Ray bothered to tape when he was on the road. He had paced the morning just right so they would arrive there in time for the well-reviewed lunch buffet. They were still fifty miles away when Mira noticed the first billboard for the place. At the top was the creed—"THE PLACE IS OASIS"— then services it had to offer: diesel, engine repair, truck wash, motel, video slots, fifty-foot buffet, pay-by-the-minute showers. And Mira could see why it was called an oasis. She spotted it from a half a mile away, huge and mustard-colored. As they took the exit, she could make out the mural of a desert scene airbrushed on its side: a camel in the shade of a lone palm tree, a cowboy-hatted man in midslide down a dune that led to a perfect circle of blue water. Ray took Aron's picture in front of the place.

Inside, they mazed through the convenience store, which doubled as the motel lobby, to the restaurant in the back. Felissa asked Aron to order her something to go and said she was going to hit the showers. When she was out of earshot, Aron told them that Felissa hadn't paid for a room at the motel, that she was just mooching off their pool. She had told Aron in the truck that morning that she hadn't showered in four days.

The restaurant was dark, just a few windows at one end and some muted light from stained-glass Budweiser lamps hanging from the ceiling. They were seated by a pear-shaped woman named Vanda. She was average-sized everywhere but her hips, where she ballooned out, and the close-fitting pants she wore accentuated that. Against her dark brown hair, even in the dim barlike light, Mira could make out the web of her hair net, meant to be invisible.

"Y'all gonna have the buffet today?" she asked. They had walked past it on their way in. The fried food in the sunken metal pans was unidentifiable, monochrome, just different shapes. Everyone opted for the menu except Kat, who got up to fill her plate.

The booth seats were upholstered with dark green carpeting—Aron said he wondered if they had been vacuumed lately—and were a little too low, so that the table came up to Mira's chest. On the wall above the table was a framed photo of Leon Russell, his arm around a man named Dewight, the owner, Mira guessed, to whom the photo was autographed in purple Magic Marker.

When Vanda came for the orders, she looked at Aron first. He asked for chicken fingers to go and a Reuben sandwich without the sauerkraut and Russian dressing.

Vanda was scratching somewhere inside her hair with the tip of her pen. "Would that make it a pastrami sandwich?"

Then Aron said back, "Would that make you a surly waitress?"

Vanda reached down and tweaked the open menu from his fingers. "I'll make the note." She took the rest of the orders and left.

Kat came back from the buffet with two plates. One was all hush puppies, and she set it in the middle of the table. "Have at it."

"Bad buffet ethics." Ray reached for one anyway.

A handsome, lanky man in heavily starched Wrangler jeans walked past the booth. Mira wondered if he was coming from the showers when he pulled a stick of deodorant out of his shirt pocket. He ripped open the first few snaps of the shirt, then slid the deodorant inside. With his arm held out at a ninety-degree angle, he stroked the deodorant on and repeated the process with the other arm. Ray caught all this, then looked at Mira.

"You think he'd let me borrow some?" Ray pointed a finger toward his own armpit. Mira enjoyed that Ray seemed to say this just to her, without looking for a laugh from Kat or Aron, as if they were alone. As he looked down to read his place-mat trivia, Mira examined his eyelashes. Darker than his hair, they could have been fake, the way they curled just right to frame his eyes. They were the kind women envied.

"Come in, Space Station Mir," Kat was saying. Mira broke her stare at Ray. Vanda had the pitcher of iced tea poised over Mira's glass, her eyebrows raised. Mira nodded. "Please."

Aron spooned ice from his water glass to his coffee. "So what do sixteen-year-olds do for amusement these days?"

"I don't know," Kat answered, bored with the question. "What do twenty-five-year-olds do?"

"Speaking for myself, I do the same things now as I did at your age."

"That's surprising." Kat held up a bite of chicken-fried steak on her fork. "Anybody want some?"

"I'll try a bite," Ray said. He reached out for her fork, but instead of handing it to him, Kat moved it toward his mouth and right up to his lips, waiting for him to open up. Mira could tell this made Ray a little antsy; he opened his mouth just enough for Kat to slide the fork in. Then his lips stayed parted as she slid the fork back out, his teeth never touching the metal. This was followed by a weird exchange of glances: Aron at Kat, Ray at Mira, Mira at Kat, Kat looking away.

This time, Mira heard Vanda coming, her polyester-clad thighs swishing together as she walked. She arrived with three plates balanced on her outstretched arm. After she had unloaded, she asked if she could get them anything else.

Aron looked inside his sandwich. "What do you call that?" He pointed to the bed of sauerkraut soaking in pink dressing.

She flipped through her tickets and found the copy of theirs. "Must be the newbies in the kitchen," she figured. "I'll get you the pastrami."

Then as she walked away, Aron muttered, "Speed it up, butter butt." At first, Mira wasn't sure whether he had said it within Vanda's earshot. Then, after everyone else was a couple of bites into their meals, a man in his fifties came out from behind swinging doors. He wore tan Sansabelt slacks that looked like they had been bought fifteen pounds ago and a plaid western-style shirt, the kind with pearlized snaps. It was Dwight.

"Couldn't you just scrape it off?" Kat asked just loud enough for Aron to hear.

Dwight came up and leaned forward with the balls of his hands resting on the table. "Y'all havin' a big time?"

"We've got our hands full with him." Ray pointed at Aron with his thumb. "Sorry about that."

"We'll just settle the bill and get going." Mira reached for her wallet.

Dwight held his hand out, palm facing Mira. "No, you're gonna leave without a meal, so consider us even." Then he stepped to the side of the table and swept his arm out in front of him, inviting them to exit. They kept quiet as they wedged out of the booth. An albino trucker in the booth behind them shook his head as he chewed, eyeing each of them as they passed.

Outside, Mira said, "Thank you for that, Aron." She spotted Felissa at the truck, still combing the tangles from her wet hair.

"Oh my God." Kat shaded her eyes as they adjusted to the sunlight. "Oh my God."

"What?" Aron held his arms out to his side. "I was bein' all normal until she started in with the pastrami bit."

Ray flicked the bill of Aron's Razorbacks cap with his middle finger, knocking it to the ground. "Piss on your pastrami."

Back in the truck, Kat decided to spend the rest of the afternoon sketching Mira's profile. The finished product looked like some colorized version of her. As Kat tried to remember what Leon Russell sang, she imagined if she were to draw Mira over the next twenty years, how the creases in her skin would multiply, the concave of her eyes would deepen, the density of her hair would slacken, and the thickness of her lips would straighten to the severe tightness that their mother's lips had taken on late in her forty-nine-year life.

 *Eight*

The first signs for Ona Island were just ten miles outside of town. Ray suggested that Mira take the lead as the turns became more frequent, the roads too obscure to show up on his atlas. They passed a WELCOME sign, a metal grating with disks attached, one for every church and civic group. A patrol car idled just behind the sign, its radar gun pointed at oncoming traffic. Ona Island had always been best known regionally as a speed trap. Tickets brought in more revenue than in any other town in western North Carolina, and the longest-serving mayors in the town's history were those who had vowed to make it statewide.

They caught all reds at the half dozen traffic lights on the main road through town. For Mira, things were beginning to look familiar, but a little off, as if she were watching a movie she had seen ten years ago. She recognized the general look of the town, but nothing was quite the way she remembered it. Now she wasn't sure whether the place had really changed that much or whether her memory of it was just askew.

"The birthplace of Kearney and Mira DeLand." Mira pointed to what had been a small hospital, now a for-profit community college. Kat's eyes trailed it as they passed. Down the road was the strip mall where Kearney had hung out; Mira had been too young. It was called University Mall, though the closest university was sixty miles away and Ona Island didn't lay any claim to it. What had been Montgomery Ward was now Art's Discount Crafts, whose sign read IF WE DON'T HAVE IT, YOU DON'T NEED IT. On either side were stores doomed to short life spans: Airbrush Studio, Everything's a Dollar, A & G Cellulars, Cryptic Comic Books, Dave's Discount Beauty Supplies. Mira's elementary school now served as the school board's office annex. The skating rink had been converted to a weekend flea market. The only gas station her parents had ever used—she had always admired their gas loyalty—had been modernized and now looked like a cartoon of a space station: a half a dozen islands, digitized gas pumps, and a neon-lit food center.

On the east end of town, Mira made a wrong turn that took them past Success Baptist Church. The sanctuary, a rectangle of stones smoothed by wind and rain, couldn't hold more than a hundred people. Its patinated steeple pointed fifty feet into the air, four times taller than the building itself. A row of trailers used as annexes sat behind the sanctuary, one for youth fellowship, one for seniors, another for singles. A portable marquee straddled the brick walkway leading to the church. In shiny block letters, it read DARWIN: SURVIVAL OF THE FITTEST . . . GOD: SURVIVAL OF THE FETUS.

As they passed the church, Mira glanced sideways at Kat to see if she could detect a reaction, any hint of recognition, knowing there was no reason to expect one. Kat's eyes were stuck on an emaciated dog, mangy and collarless, staring at them from the side of the road like a hitchhiker.

"Poor mutt," Mira said.

Kat swiveled around in her seat to watch the dog as they drove past it. "Hybrid."

Mira thought she recognized a beige Duster stopped in the left turn lane. She slowed until her light turned yellow, then pulled up next to the Duster. Right away, she knew the driver's receding chin and cap worn high enough to add a few inches to his height. It was Jim Decker, the husband of Mira's Brownie leader the couple of years before she moved away. Jim had been intense about his Airstream, which had always reminded Mira of a giant bullet. He had taken the troop camping in it a few times, but Mira's mother had pulled her out when she found out that Jim had given each kid a dozen bottle rockets to shoot off on a trip over the Fourth of July.

Mira flipped her sunglasses down and looked hard at Jim Decker. She could hear the crunch of his AM radio, his pristine Duster still quiet enough not to tune it out. He looked over at Mira, nodded blandly, and drove off.

Lila was a few miles outside of town, about a block down what had been a private road when they lived here, an unnamed and unpaved dead end. It looked more suburban now, blacktopped, houses built on every other lot. A shiny green sign marked the corner: WILMA WALKER DRIVE.

Mira came to a stop just after she made the turn, mumbled something for Kat's sake about waiting for Ray to clear it. She felt dizzy, the kind of dizziness you get when you cross your eyes and things gets swervy and remote. She tried to fight it off, focus on breathing. After a minute, when Ray started waving her ahead, she drove to the house.

There, Ray maneuvered the flatbed so that it was parallel to the street, straddling the yard and pavement. They got out of the trucks. Kat stood beside Mira at the edge of the yard, Felissa digging something out of her suitcase, Ray and Aron at the edge of the road in on-duty stances, their arms crossed, knees locked, feet a shoulder length apart.

"It looks like Dad," Kat said, almost to herself.

In no hurry, Kat just stood there, taking it in. Mira followed Kat's eyes, which were shooting around from the eaves to the triangle of wooden tiles to the dentils to the round attic window, then seemed to land on the ivy crawling up the house's face like an untamed beard. The front picture window was bare, and Mira vaguely remembered an argument between her parents over whether to board the place up. Her mother's view had won out, that boarded windows did more to encourage unlawful entry than bare ones. Looking at it now, the house seemed to have undergone a simulated age progression, its features altered but still intact, still instantly recognizable.

After a minute, they started tentatively toward the house, deciding to check out the yard first, as if they were prospective home buyers who had come upon a house for sale, hoping to be spotted and invited in. Their feet disappeared in sketchy ankle-high centipede grass and dandelions as they walked around to the right side, rotting pecans cracking under their weight. There, in the shade of a pecan tree, two rectangles the size of doors laid sideways were painted on the side of the house.

"This what they call folk art?" Aron asked.

Mira half-smiled. "They were ours."

Kat clasped her hands around the back of her neck, elbows touching. "Mom's idea?"

"Dad's. We could do whatever we wanted as long as it was inside our rectangle. Mom thought it was whimsy."

Kearney had gone through a collage phase. Crusty patches of

glue clung where there had been bark, wads of paper, dead cockroaches, locks of Mira's hair he would sneak, anything that would stick. She had preferred to think of her own as a chalkboard, make up word problems or diagram sentences in Magic Marker. To get the full effect, she would borrow her father's protective glasses, the clear plastic wraparound kind, and be sure to push them higher onto her nose with her forefinger every few seconds, as she pictured her own teachers doing. All that was left now were disconnected scribbles, profiles of imaginary people staring into the sky, or at one another, twenty versions of her name scattered over the rectangle like signatures in a yearbook. With each one, she had tried out variations in her cursive: large and loopy, then maybe small and refined, or slanted to the left. In one corner, she had written "Mr. Social Snob of 1978" and impressively drawn a dainty teacup. Why was a mystery to her now. The right half of her rectangle had been painted over where she had written a poem about being the first girl in her class to start her period, and the next day, she had come out to find a still-wet coat of paint covering it, a fresh canvas, compliments of her mother.

Ray was making his way to the backyard, which Wesley had kept as manicured as a golf green when they had lived here. Now there were only hints of that. The brick border of a flower bed, forced crooked like teeth by the wayward roots of a nearby magnolia. Bushy monkey grass still roughly in the shape of a circle. A pear tree's branches sagging with overripe pears. Rotten ones dotting the ground below, deflated or pecked with holes. Unruly wisteria vines along the back fence, twisting upward around the posts, the barbed wire, one another, anything that would hold them. The same cylinder holding a retractable clothesline bolted to the house's eave, the hook it attached to still poking out of a tree ten yards away. A picnic table—Mira couldn't remember a single picnic there—the planks now split and rotten.

Directly behind the lot was a gentle slope of several hundred feet that leveled out into flat pasture. When they had lived here, the owner had used the land to cultivate fir trees. Jes Burr advertised his Christmas-tree farm—Burr's Firs—as the "largest and firriest" in northwestern North Carolina. In the early fall, he would open his farm to customers who would tag the trees they wanted and come back to harvest them toward the holidays.

Mira remembered one year when her mother persuaded her father to help himself to a fir in the middle of the night. Mira had stood on her bed and watched from her window as they executed the plan, her mother in her terry-cloth bathrobe just on their side of the fence, advising her father in a frenzied whisper on which tree to go at with the handsaw. After a few minutes, he dragged the chosen one to the fence and the two of them lifted it over. By the time the tree was upright, leaning against the house, its branches were ruffled like feathers, and the next day, both her parents had thin scrapes like pen marks on their forearms to show for their efforts.

For locals, the understood climax to the holiday season came every New Year's night when Jes Burr hosted a tree burning. Beginning the day after Christmas, the trees would be dropped off in pickups and station wagons. By New Year's, the fragrant pile, glistening from leftover tinsel, would be as big and tall as a house, and on that night, it would burn as fiercely as one.

The DeLands had only gone to one of the tree burnings, and then only because door prizes were promised. Jes Burr and his wife—he in tails, she in a red taffeta shift—kept the crowd of a hundred or so waiting until just the right moment before emerging not from their house but from the grove of picked-over firs, as if they lived among them. After a half hour of red velvet cake, lime sherbet punch, and what Rhinetta Scanga would've called "fellowship," Jes Burr walked around the firs, tossing lit matches every few feet. The flames cracked and popped as they streamed deep into the pile like lava floes, making unexpected turns, taking their time, but soon enough enveloping everything. His work done, Jes Burr stared trancelike into the fire, standing closer than anyone else could tolerate, just a few feet away, his skin glowing orange.

The door prizes turned out to be discounts and first dibs on next year's trees, which ticked Helen off, so on the way home, she went on about how Jes Burr looked like the devil, and if not that, then at least he was big on himself. They never went back, but every New Year's night, Mira waited at her bedroom window for the orange sheen to appear in the sky and looked forward to the luxurious smell of fir and cinder that would linger in town for days.

Now the firs had been replaced by tobacco plants, waist-high and by the thousands. Their leaves rattled in the slight breeze.

Mira didn't notice that Ray had left the backyard until he came back and pulled her by the elbow up close to the house. Kat was with Aron and Felissa, who were poking around the tobacco leaves, Aron nabbing a few for himself.

"Get rid of Kat." Ray twitched his eyes toward the tobacco.

Mira waited for the joke. "What are you on?"

"Get her to the motel," he said through almost-clenched teeth. He guided Mira toward Kat, his hand pressing into the small of her back. Mira felt herself smile dumbly, trying to look casual.

"Maybe y'all go check in." Mira waved in the direction of the trucks. "We'll be there shortly."

Without meaning to, Aron helped her out. "We can see what

amenities await at the Holidome." Wayne Gaar's secretary had made reservations for the next two nights.

"But I want the tour," Kat said.

"I need to putter around the house first, sort through some of the junk." This was the best Mira could come up with, but Kat surrendered more easily than Mira expected.

Kat fanned herself with the tobacco leaf she had picked. "Putter away."

"We'll meet you there later," Ray said. Aron and Felissa, pinkies linked, started for his pickup, Kat following them. Like an afterthought, Ray tossed Aron his cell phone and told him to call Wayne, tell him they'd made it okay.

After they left, Mira jogged behind Ray toward the front of the house, asking what was wrong as they went, getting no answer. Mira had the key ready, but when they got to the front porch, she saw that the knob hung down limp against the door.

"Been pried open." Ray nudged the knob with the tail of his shirt. The latch bolt was lodged inside, so there was nothing to catch the door closed. Mira tapped on the door, and it swung open with no resistance. In an instant, they both caught a rotten whiff from inside.

Mira started to go in, but Ray cupped his hand around her wrist. "Wait here." Mira hoped she would remember this bit of protectiveness later, when she could enjoy it with undivided attention.

Ray sucked in air, pursed his mouth, and went inside, pushing the door to behind him. Mira heard the knock of his boots against the hardwood floor as he went from the living room to the kitchen, then down the hallway to the rear bedroom. The footsteps stopped when he got to the master bedroom, which was carpeted.

After a few seconds, when nothing happened, Mira pushed the

door open with her shoe and started inside. Her eyes landed on the sofa, the only piece of living room furniture they had left behind—she couldn't remember why. By instinct, she walked over and lifted up the two cushions, revealing a tortoiseshell button, a wheat penny, and a crumpled strip of Green Stamps. She looked closer and spotted a few nearly invisible hairs, and though she knew it was spooky, she wanted to examine each one, identify it, try to imagine the exact moment at which it fell or was pulled out and found its place in the time capsule under the sofa cushion.

Remembering Ray, Mira followed the slow knock of his boots against the hallway floor. The air seemed to get thick, as if it carried bits of decay and she was sucking them into her lungs with each uneven breath, doing herself in. Though she had never smelled a dead body, Mira suddenly knew with odd certainty that that was what Ray had found.

Mira walked into the master bedroom. The dead man, who looked to be in his seventies, lay diagonally across the bed, his yellowed undershirt riding midway up his stomach, kneeless jeans unbuttoned but still zipped. His bare and blackened feet stuck off the corner of the bed, heels together, toes pointed out like a V. His eyes had sunk into their sockets, skin taken on the colors of a bruise.

Ray stood at the foot of the bed and palmed the crown of his head. The warning signs of vomiting hit Mira in quick waves: her mouth watered, stomach burned, then her throat. All this gained momentum as she rushed toward the bathroom, only realizing this wouldn't do when she crouched over the empty toilet, its receding water stains like rings on a tree stump, reminding her that years had passed.

She left the bathroom, running now, and palmed open the front door, half conscious of the instantly familiar sound of footsteps on the porch, then made it to the grass just in time. In a minute, she felt Ray kneel behind her. He held her hair back and handed her a bandanna to wipe her face with.

Afterward, Mira sat on the steps, and Ray took a seat behind her with his legs parted. He nudged her to lean into him. She did, and he tilted his head down to look at her, then looked away.

They sat there for a few minutes, not saying anything. Mira concentrated on the feel of the trusty clean air as she breathed it in, the coolness of it against her skin, which was clammy, as if she'd just broken a fever. She noticed how the view from the porch was different, less sky, more spines of pine tress not quite parallel to one another, like the teeth of an old comb.

Mira looked at Ray. "I'd been looking forward to smelling the house, seeing if it smelled the same."

"What did it used to smell like?"

"I don't know." She clutched at her knees with webbed hands. "A million things."

Then Ray said, "I've never been to a funeral."

Mira flicked a roly-poly off the toe of his boot. "Not even a grandparent's?"

"I only knew one of my grandparents, and he lived half a continent away."

"Had you ever seen a dead person?"

"Saw one under a sheet once," he said. "At the Little Rock airport. I was picking Liz up, and this guy on her plane had a heart attack and died right there in coach. A couple of jollies wheeled the guy off on a stretcher, carrying on like it was a dessert tray. All you could see were his running shoes, but under the sheet, his stomach stuck up like a basketball." Then Ray looked down at Mira, waiting for her answer to the same question.

"My Dad. He died in his sleep. And my mother."

"How'd she die?"

Mira had picked up an azalea leaf and was tracing her forefinger along its veins and midrib. "A stroke."

Then Ray asked Mira what her mother was like, but the question got lost, because he was webbing his fingers through her hair, pulling it up toward him, then letting it fall back down in weightless layers. After a minute of this, he started braiding a lock near her right temple. She enjoyed the mild tug of his fingers.

Mira let her eyes float shut. "Where'd you learn to braid?"

"Who can't braid?" Ray said back.

"I bet Liz taught you."

When he didn't say anything, Mira cocked her head back and opened her eyes.

He sent her what she thought was a faint smile, though they were looking at each other upside down, so she couldn't quite read his face, whether he was thinking about Liz, maybe tracing the outline of Mira's lips, or just intent on the braiding, which he was still busy at. He glanced at Mira, and she shut her eyes and froze his stare there.

A couple of minutes later, when he had reached the end of the strands, he leaned down toward her, his jeans scratching against the concrete step. She kept her eyes closed but could feel his breath on her forehead, then the brush of his lips there.

Mira and Ray went in search of a phone, tried the place next door, a mobile home weighted down by a dozen tires on its roof. No one answered. At the end of the driveway, Mira picked up one of a scattering of blue rubber bands to wrap around the end of the braid, then they walked a couple of lots down the road.

They stopped at one of the newer houses, this one Spanish mission–style. A grid of new sod squares had just been laid out, and as they stepped onto the porch, the place smelled like Lowe's. A fiftyish woman came to the door holding a yapping Chihuahua in one arm and a spirit level in the other. Her gray hair was twisted back into a severe bun that pulled her skin tight across her face, and Mira wondered if that was the idea.

"Hushie, Pooker." She puckered her lips at the dog, which continued its racket. "Can I help you?"

"I'm an owner from down the street. We've got . . ." Mira fumbled with how much to say. "Mind if we use your phone?"

She looked back over her shoulder. "If I can find it," she said, smiling.

They walked through the foyer into a den that didn't quite look lived in, just a sectional couch and two end tables with nothing on them. A half dozen pictures leaned against walls. Another half dozen were already hung. Several were heirloom portraits, the kind seen over mantels or at the head of staircases. The largest, about the size of a card table, was of the woman looking ten years younger but sporting the same hair bun, her cocked arm holding Pooker just as it was now.

She handed Ray a cordless phone and motioned for him to sit down on the couch, but he stayed put. The woman's eyes perked up when she heard him dial only three numbers.

"Yes, I'm at . . ." He raised his eyebrows at Mira.

"The last road on the left off of Nesting Place before the dead end," Mira prompted.

"Wilma Walker Drive," the woman said, flashing Mira a funny look. Ray repeated this into the phone.

"I'm a mover, just arrived with the owner to move a home." He spoke quietly, as if this would lessen the shock for the woman. "There's a deceased in the residence."

The woman jerked her hand to her mouth, then pulled Pooker's face to hers, as if he, too, would be hit hard by the news.

"About ten minutes ago," Ray was saying into the phone. "Thank you." He pushed the off button. "Say they'll be here shortly."

"I knew that freak house was bad news." The woman sat down on the couch, holding Pooker with one hand, rubbing the other in small controlled circles around her kneecap, looking straight ahead.

"Let's go keep a watch out," Ray said.

"Thanks for the phone." Mira kept her eyes on the woman as they left, sorry to leave her like that, and wondering if she would go back to the pictures.

By the time they had walked to the pickup, they could already hear the whine of sirens. An ambulance came first, followed by a small convoy of police cars. Ray walked toward the house to lead the paramedics to the body. All the cops followed them but one, a middle-aged man in a heavily starched white shirt with loosened tie. In one liquid motion, as if it had been part of his training, he flicked his wallet open with a snap of his wrist, displaying his badge, just as he reached his other hand out to shake Mira's.

"I'm Detective R. Watkins." Despite the semiprofessional dress, he had a greasy look that she suspected stayed with him all the time, not just on the most severe summer days. Excess saliva bubbled at the corners of his mouth.

"I'm Mira DeLand."

For the next fifteen minutes, he questioned her about what she had seen, whether they had touched or moved the body or anything in the house, how long the house had been unoccupied, whether it had changed hands, who maintained the yard. He typed her answers into a note-taking calculator contraption the size of an index card, tapping one letter at a time with his forefinger, twice asking her to slow down. She could hear windows opening up at the house.

After the inquiry, R. Watkins rubbed her upper arm with the outside of his fingers. "I know this is one of those hard to swallow things, Miss DeLand. We do have a counselor with the Police Department who's trained for crises such as these." Mira unkindly imagined a classroom full of police officers attending a lecture series over brown-bag lunches. Today's topic: "Appropriate Displays of Sympathy Toward Trauma Victims."

"This isn't my first crisis," Mira told him, "but thanks." He slid his Notekeeper into his shirt pocket and hiked his pants up as he walked toward the house.

Mira sat on the tailgate of the pickup until they wheeled the body out. She could see the man's outline through the opaque body bag, his hands folded on his stomach as if he were napping. The seams and cracks in the driveway jolted the stiffened body.

Ray must have been interviewed inside, because all of the cops left as soon as he came out, R. Watkins saying that they had collected what they needed to from the scene and they would call for a follow-up.

He gave her a thumbs-up before he left. "Have a good one." Easy on the enthusiasm, Mira thought.

Ray decided to take the long way back to the motel in the pickup, leaving the rig at the house for the next day's move. As he drove, he feigned interest in the right side of the road, instead catching glances of Mira from behind his sunglasses, which he had stopped needing two hours ago. He was thinking about how she looked beautiful without even trying, how makeup worked against a face like hers, how her lean, tan hands came to rest on the inside of her thighs, pressed between them, how lovely they looked there.

Fifteen minutes later, Ray reversed into a parking space at the motel, then asked Mira if they could just sit there for a minute. Without answering, she shifted down and around in her seat to face him, leaning her head back. It was almost dark. The parking lot's lights were just now fading on.

"So are we gonna keep this to ourselves?" Mira asked.

"I'd say it would tarnish the house for Kat."

Mira was fiddling with a receipt she had found in the seat, folding it in half as many times as she could. "I have the urge to tell you something."

"Tell away." Ray suddenly felt nervous, then embarrassed at himself for being nervous. When she hesitated, Ray said, "You know you're gonna end up telling me."

"My mother had an affair with our minister when we lived here."

Ray shifted down lower in his seat. "Is that why you moved?" Mira nodded. "So why'd you keep the house?"

"My Dad built it, which I know doesn't sound like much of a reason to someone who didn't know my father."

Mira tossed the receipt to the floor, then started rotating the knob on the gearshift. Ray studied her hand, the way each knuckle looked like a small Adam's apple and the veins merged in between them. Except for a half-moon scar on her index finger, it was perfect, like a hand would be drawn.

"I can't sleep." Ray tried to catch her eye, wondering how she would take this.

"I brought a thermos of Wiederkehr's wine," she said, and Ray figured she could tell right away from the look on his face what a nice idea he thought this was, the idea of drinking wine with her. Then Mira added, "That might help knock you out." And it was embarrassingly clear to him then that her offer of wine had been no more an overture than if she had handed him an over-the-counter sleep aid.

"That'll do."

Back in her room, Mira evaluated her split-second decision to play dumb to Ray's insomnia claim. She replayed the look on his face, a look that said he wished she had taken it as a joke, the way his lips pursed and his stare was drawn sideways to some imaginary point that suddenly demanded his attention. She remembered Marcus once offering her the legal explanation of separation he had gotten from a lawyer buddy he was always quoting. He had said that if the two people maintain separate residences, then the separation is legal and sleeping with someone else isn't technically adultery. Mira wondered now if this was true, if there'd even been such a lawyer buddy, or if Marcus had just had his eye on a sweet-faced coed he wanted to take home and show his maps to.

Knowing Ray was stuck in the room now with Aron and Felissa, that if she hauled him back out for some sleep-inducing activity that they would probe for an explanation, Mira resigned herself to watching an old episode of *What's Happening* with Kat, the one where Rerun gets caught bootlegging a Doobie Brothers concert. During the commercials, she thumbed through the Ona Island phone book, which was combined with two adjacent towns and still no thicker than the owner's manual to her Honda. There were no more Bleechers.

She couldn't think of anyone else to look up, which for an instant she found terribly depressing. Then she turned to the *C*'s and found a listing for Dr. Don Case, her former dentist and the subject of her first crush. He had filled every cavity she had ever gotten, and she could recall the circumstances of each one as if they had been kisses. During her last visit before the move, after Dr. Case had filled two cavities, the hygienist stepped out to get Mira's complimentary toothbrush. She could remember wondering if he had planned this, because right after the woman left, he grinned and said, "I guess it's just you and me." Mira had wanted to say something back, send him the perfect reply, but her mouth was deadened from the bubble gum–flavored anesthetic he had rubbed on her gums with his gloved finger. So she just smiled, shifting her stare between his eyes and her own expression, which was reflected in the plastic shield covering his face. As her mother drove her home in the Fury that day, Mira slid the toothbrush out of its box, and when she saw that it was inscribed with Dr. Case's name, she vowed never to brush with it, and held true to this, only to find her mother using it to scrub the mildew off the tub's caulking some months later.

Something drew Mira's eyes back to the TV. The graphic floating to the left of the night anchor—a pretty woman with what had to be natural red hair—was a white-on-black chalk outline of a dead body, limbs bent and head cocked. Kat had the remote control, and she made the connection before Mira did. The house flashed on the screen, then trembly footage of the man's body being wheeled on a gurney from the ambulance to the morgue, then a clip from an interview with R. Watkins. He had tightened his tie and put on a dark blue jacket. Evidently, a charitable handler had wiped the crusted saliva from the corners of his mouth.

"No next of kin has been found as of this time." He shut his eyes into a quick squint. "There was a life lost in that house, the circumstances of which we know not."

Kat turned off the TV and leaned up on her elbows, looking straight at Mira. "Was that the junk you wanted to sort through?"

"I wasn't sure what to do," Mira said lamely.

"So you decided not to tell me."

"I just hadn't decided yet." Mira wished she could do better.

"Are you trying to assume the parent role here?"

"I don't know about assuming."

"This just in: I'm past the dribbling stage."

"It had nothing to do with us. He was after shelter. It could've been any house."

"So the rule is that you tell me things that have to do with us, and those that don't, you decide not to fuzzy me up with."

"Is that a good rule?"

"I think a dead man found in our house has to do with us. I think that counts." And when Kat said this, it sounded to Mira like the most obvious thing in the world, and she wondered how she could've thought otherwise a few hours earlier.

"Are you sure you're not really twenty-six?" Mira asked.

And then after a pause, Kat said out of nowhere, "Ray's manly."

"Thank God. You're talking your age. Say something else."

"So you're too evolved to think Ray's manly?"

Mira flipped off the light. "Night, Stanley." And after Mira mumbled to Kat that she loved her, and Kat mumbled, "Ditto," Mira lay there knowing she had gotten caught, that she had dodged a close one, and amazed at how on target Kat was about things.

Mira went to sleep with the arrogant feeling that she had been part of something adult, heartbreaking, larger than life, something that would be recorded on its own by some transcendental date keeper, the same one that records reasons for noteless suicides, the ambitions and regrets of voiceless animals, and volcanic eruptions on uninhabited islands so remote that the most thorough cartographers have overlooked them.

 *Nine*

Mira awoke from a deep motel sleep to the yelps of unruly kids and smallish dogs next door; she couldn't tell one from the other. Kat somehow slept through it, lying diagonally across her bed, all cocooned in the covers except for her enviably dainty bare feet, which poked off the side. The AC had been on all night. Mira woke up cold-nosed to find the room about sixty degrees.

She slid on yesterday's jeans and a clean T-shirt. Aron's truck was gone, so she checked for a message at the front desk. Ray had written one on Holiday Inn stationery: "We're at the house. Ray." Even his handwriting had charisma, printed in all caps, uniform and boxy.

Kat and Mira ate single-serving boxes of Raisin Bran at a table in a rectangle of similar ones in the motel lobby. The place had been given a countrified look, lots of dusty blues and wooden teddy bear wall hangings. Along with some retirees, a dozen or so sports fishermen ate at the other tables, the backs of their thick necks sunburned the color of boiled lobster shells, a stark contrast to their crisp white T-shirts advertising the fishing rodeo Mira figured they were in town for.

"Mom should be here." Kat grinned, pointing her spoon toward the fishermen. By their mother's design, no one in the family had been fishing since they had left North Carolina. Mira remembered once being asked by a surly girl in her class why her father and brother didn't fish, as if it were a sign that her family was fundamentally askew. When Mira told her that it was for humanitarian reasons—the only excuse she could conjure in an instant—the girl looked at Mira as if her suspicions had been confirmed.

A beefy man standing at a coffee machine said to the woman he was with, "We have an issue, you and me." As Kat and Mira made the drive to the house, they took turns speculating about what this issue might be: too little sex, too many shopping sprees, too much cream, not enough sugar.

The stretch of road in front of the house was like a truck retrospective: antiques with contoured hoods and wheel wells, bland squared-off Fords from the seventies, rusting Datsuns with camper tops, Chevy Luvs that looked like toys next to the others. Then there were the latest models. From the outside, they had been made to mimic the older ones, only larger, but their insides were as plush and digitized as Jack Scanga's Continental.

Ray's flatbed was where he had left it yesterday. Mira didn't spot Felissa but saw Aron and Ray among a dozen hard-hatted men standing motionless in a semicircle around the forty-foot pine tree, its armlike branches folded as if daring them to come any closer. When Ray saw Mira and Kat, he stepped backward, away from the group.

A couple of tools Mira couldn't identify hung from loops on his canvas work pants, chiming as he walked. He wore a faded red T-shirt that looked like it had been washed a hundred times. It lay smoothly against his chest in the loveliest way.

"We've got a glitch." He pointed to the pine. "How attached are you?"

"I was never into that initial-carving thing."

"If it's worth it to you, we can salvage the wood."

Kat twirled her index finger in a sarcastic circle. "I can carve my bust out of it."

Ray twitched his shoulders. "Or you could sell it to a lumberyard for a hundred bucks."

"Good luck yanking it out," Mira said.

"Okay if we sacrifice the azaleas, too?"

Mira's father had planted a row of them along the front of the house, just under the picture window. Mira nodded.

"So can we go inside?" Kat asked.

Ray shook his head. "We've already got the doors secured." Kat mouthed a sarcastic *Okay*.

Ray megaphoned that an alley twenty by fifty feet needed to be cleared to the west of the tree. The men left their huddle and re-arranged the trucks. Ray pulled the flatbed up in front of the next lot. Then a small man started toward the tree with a chain saw, everyone clearing out of his way, as if this were his jurisdiction. With one jerk of the cord, the thing coughed to a start. He stood with knees bent, back straight, arms still, his stance as studied as a pro golfer's, preparing to drive. His wrists did all the work, cocking back and forth to guide the saw, which seemed a natural extension of his hands as he edged into the tree's blond core. The scene reminded Mira of a lumberjack rodeo on ESPN: hunky, bearded, flannel-clad men racing to saw through tree trunks, climbing retired telephone poles, shuffling their feet to stay balanced on floating logs.

Though it wasn't yet ten o'clock, the air was already sticky. Sweat dripped from the tip of the man's nose. Ovals of sweat soaked his shirt at the armpits. He kept this up for about twenty minutes, until the tree cracked a final time and made a lazy descent, just as they had expected, into the path that had been cleared for it. When it hit the ground, small branches snapped inside the larger ones and brittle pinecones bounced free like Ping-Pong balls. Then, Aron and a Burt Convey look-alike spent the next hour working to attach the tree to a harness, then drag it out of the way behind one of the trucks.

Mira walked over to a skinny man in a hard hat who seemed to be playing the part of supervisor, told him she was the owner, and asked whether there was anything she could take care of in the meantime.

He wore a pinkie ring, the kind with a rough face of gold nuggets, which accentuated the way his pinkie stayed separate from the other fingers as he raised a coffee cup to his mouth. After a loud sip and without looking her in the eye, he said, "Got a magic wand?"

Dejected, Mira spent the next hour watching the maneuvering from the bed of the truck parked across the street. Hydraulic lifts had already been positioned about every ten feet along the sides and back of the house. Pairs of crewmen were drilling holes into the house's base, then inserting steel beams in each one. The men struck Mira as being like worker ants, intent and focused, like they had found their jackpot habitat but it had to be moved to a less hostile environment, so they had organized into a tiny chain of command, each one playing some ant part in the moving of this vital thing.

After a while, Ray walked over holding a paper cone of water.

"You've got hard-hat hair," Mira said. It was damp with sweat and pressed close to his head.

"Damn, and our on-location hairdresser's at a perm convention."

"A shame."

Ray gave her a long look, his elbows leaning on the truck's frame. In the hazy light, his skin glowed a little, misted from the heat. "Aron looked her over inside. There's not enough furniture to worry about, so he roped what's there to screws drilled into the foundation."

"Sounds good," she said. "So'd you sleep okay?"

"Fair to middlin'. The peroxide made for funky dreams."

"Peroxide?"

Ray nodded toward Aron. "Wait till he takes the hard hat off. Felissa spent half the night giving him a dye job. He's stiffing me because I told him he looked like a cupcake."

"Where is she?"

"Sleeping in."

"Aron must be smitten." Mira waved a fly away. "What were the sleeping arrangements?"

"He was Mr. Gentleman, gave her the bed and slept on the floor." Ray swiped the sweat from his face with his shoulder. "How'd you sleep?"

"I had a dream myself. It's fuzzy, something about a dead man . . ."

Ray took a sip from his cone. "Did you have breakfast?"

"Continental."

Mira was taken by Ray's mundane questions about her felt needs—food, shelter, and the rest. She found this concern of his flattering; whether he intended it that way didn't matter at the moment.

"Anybody mention yesterday?" she asked.

"Aron saw the news and got a little freaked out, asked all about what the man looked like, whether his eyes were open. He made me lie on the bed exactly how the guy was when we found him, the look on his face and everything."

"That's creepy."

"I spooked myself. Then Felissa went off on morticians."

"Kat saw it, too, before I came to my senses."

"How'd that go over?"

"She thinks I should've told her."

Ray used his finger to wipe the freckles of sweat from his nose. "Your intentions were good." He paused. "One of the guys asked if he could have the azalea bushes, says his wife could use 'em."

"She's a lucky lady."

Ray smiled, and Mira smiled back, a big, foolish smile, one she couldn't have stifled if she'd tried.

Someone whistled for Ray, then yelled that they were ready for him to back the flatbed up to the house. As Ray walked away, his feet swishing in the sketches of crispy grass, Mira could tell from the curve of his face from her angle that the smile was still there.

Ray maneuvered the flatbed into position, just a couple of feet away from the front porch. Then he made his way around the house, checking the steel beams and the placement of the hydraulic jacks, each of which was about waist-high and looked from where Mira was like a cluster of steel cylinders standing upright. Ray called for some adjustment of the jacks, and when it was made, each one let out a vibrating hum that reminded Mira of the sound of her father's air compressor.

Within a few seconds, almost undetectably, the house was raised like a car on a garage lift, but much more slowly. The ivy on all sides was stretched from its roots, each vine breaking in two like human hair. The crew's eyes shot back and forth between the jacks and Ray, who was standing on the end of the flatbed. Everyone was all business, acting in perfect sync, their lips pursed and faces stoic, like pallbearers.

When the jacks had lifted the house about four feet off the ground, Ray got into the cab of his truck. As he backed up, two crewmen on each side guided him with hand signals like third-base coaches. The truck inched under the house with less than a foot to spare. When the house's face was almost to the front of the flatbed, Ray got out and circled the house again, using a retracting tape measure to make sure it was centered.

Then the process was reversed. The crew released enough pressure in the jacks for the house to be lowered onto the bed. The jacks' hum took on a slight whistle, like a deflating balloon. Ray was standing just off to the side, calling out directions, Mira figured, though she couldn't make out what he was saying. Afterward, the steel beams were slid out and the jacks pulled clear of the house.

Mira hadn't noticed that Kat was gone until she walked back toward the pickup. "Where'd you wander to?"

"End of the street and back." Kat sat on the open tailgate and stared at the house, suddenly absorbed in the moving of it, as if she hadn't noticed it until now.

The crew was clustering around an orange watercooler resting on an open tailgate. Mira decided to go for a closer look at the house and walked over to its right side. The rectangles were exposed in full view, out of the shadow and clutter of the pecan tree. Looking at them now, they struck her as either too personal to be out there or too silly—she wasn't sure which.

Under the flatbed, between the tires, Mira could see the

foundation left behind, as pristine as if it had just been poured. She stepped up to look at the front right corner. Her father had traced his initials into the concrete, in cursive and all caps.

After a break, Ray and Aron began anchoring the house to the flatbed with strands of chain about two feet long, each one with a large hook on either end. Eyes for the hooks had already been drilled into the house's frame. Mira overheard a flirtatious crewman explaining to Kat that the chains were just in case of a jackknife, that the weight of the house would keep it from going anywhere under normal driving conditions.

After the house was secured, Ray said he and Aron were going to stick around to help load up the jacks, then stop at the subcontractor's office "to settle up with them." Mira and Kat said they would meet them at the motel. As they left, Mira got her first look at Aron's hair. Except for a few stars of brown left at the roots, it was some cross between yellow and blond.

Ray saw her looking. "Beaten Egg number thirty-six."

Kat was silent in the pickup as they headed back, not pouting, just reluctant to look Mira's way or say much of anything. She swiveled the rearview mirror around to examine her sunburn. It was already pink and would be worse after a shower and a couple of hours, Mira figured. Kat pressed a thumb into her cheek, then watched the white spot left behind, the way it turned back to pink after a second or two. This nonchalance seemed forced, and Mira wondered if something about the house had caught her off guard.

Back in the room, just wanting to test her mood, Mira said, "Want me to run and get some aloe?"

Kat had taken off everything but her T-shirt and climbed into bed, though it was still afternoon. "I have some breaking news."

"What is it?" Mira knew she would imagine the worst if given the time.

"Today I talked to a woman Dad knew."

"A woman?" Mira repeated dumbly. Kat reached for her shorts on the floor and pulled an envelope from the back pocket.

"Aron found this in the house this morning. I guess he saw me before you."

"Wesley" was written on the front of the envelope. Inside was a piece of stationery that looked like a doily. It read:

Wesley,

I know if you're reading this, Ellen is gone. Please come by.

Lila

The date was written in the top right corner—January 9, 1989—and below that, a phone number. Mira read it again, twice. Her eyes stuck on the names. She slid it back into the envelope. "You talked to her?"

"That's the walk I went for," Kat said. "I borrowed the neighbor's phone."

"The Chihuahua?" Mira asked. Kat nodded, rolling her eyes. "What do you mean she knew Dad?"

"I think 'close friend' were her words." Kat had knocked the covers off and was popping her toe knuckles one at a time.

"Why would she tell you that?"

"I said I was you. I knew she'd tell me more."

"She must've heard about Dad."

"She hadn't until I told her."

Mira hung her head back between her shoulder blades. "Why did you decide to tell me, not just let it go?"

Kat shot Mira a look that said it was a stupid question. "Kind of a big thing to just let go." Then after a pause, she added, "Plus, she said she wanted to meet me. You, I mean."

"How was it left?"

"That if I could meet her, I'd call."

As far as Mira knew, the most scandalous thing her father had ever done was fail to report some of the earnings from his business consulting inventors. Excessive taxation had always been his pet issue; all the fathers she had ever known had had one. Whenever the subject came up, her father would launch into diatribes against the federal government, and she would count the seconds until his neck patched red and his nostrils flared. But he'd been especially passionate about the business he started on his own, "his brainchild," he called it. When it came to talking about that, his pinched nerve would act up, and her mother would see to it that he spent an extra half hour in the neck stretcher that day. "It goes against the capitalist grain," Mira had heard him say a dozen times. The IRS had never called him on his tax practices, and though she figured his omissions were illegal, they seemed to be carried out in the best spirit.

Mira picked up the phone and dialed the number on the note. It took several rings for a woman with a pretty voice to answer. "Hello?" Mira's panic finger pushed the button to hang up the phone. She mumbled a fusion of several curses, which came out unrecognizable. Kat laughed from the other bed as she flipped the channels on the TV.

Mira dialed again. The woman answered within a ring. "Yes?" She wavered her voice in irritation.

"Is Monty there?"

"Check your number, sweetie." Mira hung up and pinched the bridge of her nose.

"You're not asking her out on a date." Kat stopped the TV on a courtroom sketch—from a local murder trial, the voice-over said. "Look at that crap. Those are one step above stick figures."

In a minute, Mira dialed again, and this time the woman picked up before Mira even heard it ring. "Confound it, what?" she said. Mira gave herself a second for this to sink in. *Confound it* had been her father's favorite profanity—if it counted as one—though he had always been selective about when to use it, which had seemed to enhance its effect.

"Is this Lila?"

"This is she. May I ask who's calling?"

"It's Mira Deland."

"Mira," she said, maybe surprised Mira was calling again, or wondering why her voice sounded different from the way it had earlier in the day.

"Sorry for my hang-ups," Mira said. "I wasn't too sure about calling you back." They were speaking in between pauses, as if on an international line.

"Can I see you?"

Somehow, that Lila asked first, even though Mira had called, made Mira think had Lila had something at stake in this, something to lose if they didn't meet, or to gain if they did. She sounded desperate. Poised but desperate.

They arranged to meet that night. This worked out well, as it turned out, because Aron and Ray had been invited to a pig picking

by the tree guy. As a child, Mira had been to one sponsored by the
Ona Island Chamber of Commerce, arrived just in time to catch
the pig squirming before it was skewered. When asked why it was
necessary to use a live pig, the pit master had said, "Makes for a
juicier pork."

Mira was prepared to argue that Kat shouldn't go with her, but
Kat surprised her when she said, "I'd rather chew on tin foil." When
Ray and Aron asked Felissa and Kat to go with them, Kat said that
would tickle her pinker than a pig in mud.

Mira recognized Lila's house right away. That it looked familiar
didn't in itself seem that strange, and she tried not to read anything
into it. She figured that was part of living in a small town. Each
house becomes a sort of landmark. You start to recognize the cars
in the driveway, the way they're parked, the boats and RVs covered
with blue tarps off to the side, the yard-maintenance habits of the
owner. It all becomes part of the scenery.

Mira remembered driving by the house as a child, feeling min-
iature next to the fountain out front and the steep marble staircase
that led up to the first of two stories, guarded on either side by
sculpted life-size lions, paws eternally crossed. It was the closest
thing to Graceland she had ever seen.

Now, the house looked modest, almost sad, as if it also knew
that it wasn't what it wanted to be. The marble staircase turned out
to be concrete. The fountain Mira remembered on the grassy island
between the circular drive and the road was actually a birdbath. The
life-size lions were, in fact, terra-cotta miniatures that could have
been bought at a garden center along with cheap lattice and peat

moss. As a child, she had known next to nothing about the family that lived here, just that they owned the town's only car dealership and IGA.

Mira parked halfway around the circular drive. Up the steps, she knocked and the door opened instantly, as if Lila's hand had been poised on the knob. Lila seemed about her father's age, maybe mid-fifties, and was dressed in the understated way that wealthy people tend toward, all beige and white linen. Her longish gray-blond hair, ebbing and flowing as she moved, matched the color of her skin, which made her deep blue eyes harder to miss. She had the look of an outmoded movie star, one beyond her prime but still revered. She was beautiful.

"Mira," Lila said as she waved her in. Mira smelled citrus and White Shoulders as she shook Lila's hand, which felt small, almost weightless. She led her into a formal living room, the kind in which lots of money is invested but little time is spent. This one went to extremes. Each painting had its own oblong spotlight arcing up toward it. The couch and two chairs, upholstered with velvet the color of avocado, were sheathed in thick plastic slipcovers that fit snugly, as if they had been custom-ordered. A clear rubber runner extended over the main stretch of carpet, cutting the room in half.

"Normally, I'm not such a clean queen," Lila said, excusing the oddness. "I've got grandkids coming in tomorrow." She spoke with the mildest twang, just a hint of one, the kind that news anchors occasionally let slip, despite their training to the contrary.

A large plastic bowl full of oranges sat on top of a vinyl tablecloth in the middle of the floor. A smaller bowl held peeled oranges. Peel scraps lay in a discard pile. Lila took a seat on the floor, cross-legged in front of the setup.

"I admit to a phobia of store-bought orange juice," she said. "This relaxes me, anyway."

When Mira didn't say anything, Lila added, "Good source of folate, too." The silence seemed to bother her. "Feel free to join me." Mira sat on a free corner of the tablecloth and started peeling. Lila went on. "I suppose I was a little vague today. Left you guessing."

"I have some guesses." Mira knew this sounded curt, like she was trying to make her squirm, which wasn't the plan. It was not that Mira didn't have anything to say, more like she didn't know which thing to start with.

"I can tell you I was not your father's lover."

The word *lover* sounded harsh coming from her, somehow more graphic than Mira was ready for.

Lila went on. "It's not the kind of thing I can prove, but even if I had sordid secrets about your father, I'd have no reason to tell them to you."

"Then why couldn't you mail the letter to his house?" Just then, a bullet of juice from the orange Mira was peeling shot Lila in the eye. She shriveled her lid into a squint. "Sorry," Mira mumbled.

"I wrote that letter last night, took it over to the house." Lila blinked the one eye. "I saw the story on the news, that the house was about to be moved by its owner. It was my mistake to assume that the owner would still be Wesley." She studied Mira's peeling technique. "Try to get off as much vein as you can."

"Why did you date it 1989?"

"Same reason you hung up on me twice today. I panicked. Until last night, I'd heard no mention of him, no word from him since you moved away. I didn't know whether his marriage was still intact. I felt like I had waited too long to try to find out. So I dated it 1989. There's nothing magic about that year, just that it was years before now."

Mira was peeling blind, staring at a portrait framed above the mantel. It was of a serviceman, maybe in his thirties. His features looked touched up, idealized: eyes too blue, eyebrows too combed, cheeks blushed at just the right angle, lips pink and shiny. He looked like a doll.

"How did you know my dad?"

After a few seconds, Lila put down the orange she was working on and tore a paper towel from the roll next to her. She wiped her hands. Then, as if she had been expecting the question, she reached to a nearby table for a photograph and handed it to Mira.

"He built this house." The photo was small and square, the colors washed out. Wesley and Lila sat on stacks of concrete mix bags, Lila wearing a long, flowy thing, Wesley in his work clothes, hard hat in his lap. He was sitting like he had more often than not, legs crossed, hands pressed between them. He seemed to be in mid-sentence, Lila listening.

"I was captivated by your father. He by me, too, and had it been up to me, there would've been an affair, but he refused." Lila went back to the peeling as she talked. "He was your mother's devotee. But your father and I became close friends. He'd come by several afternoons a week. We'd just talk, drink tea; he'd bring over the daily crossword, which became a bit of an addiction with us. We got to where we'd make up our own clues, just use the grid, end up infuriated. Anyway, whenever I tried to push things along, which I admit to doing, your father would go on about Ellen and you and Kearney and end up in a fit of tears. He blew me away with that."

"It's Helen," Mira said.

But Lila's face had already gone limp, and for the next minute she seemed to forget Mira was there, her hands frozen in midpeel, her glassy eyes aimed off to the side, trancelike. Then, just as suddenly, she snapped out of it.

"Despite my intentions, it was harmless as it could've been," she said. "Friends is all he let us be."

"Why'd you want to see me?" Mira asked.

"Selfish reasons, I guess. I wanted to see something of Wes. He could've been my husband of thirty years, I miss him so much." She was putting the scraps in the bowl for unpeeled oranges, now empty. "And for what it's worth coming from me, I wanted you to know that he adored all of you."

It wasn't so much the way she said this but the fact of what she said that hit Mira the wrong way, as if Lila was doing her a favor she didn't want.

They sat there until the chime of an out-of-sight clock seemed to call attention to the silence. Mira thought it was to break the stalemate that Lila split a peeled orange and gave her half. And as they passed a cup back and forth to spit the seeds into, all Mira could think was that it should've felt stranger than it did.

The orange eaten, Mira got up from the floor and reached for her purse. Then Lila said, "First come see."

They passed through a combination door—just like the ones her father had built into their own house—and went into the dining room. Lila led her to a pie safe, in its door hundreds of tiny holes arranged in the shape of a pie. Inside were three shelves of preserves in mason jars, a label stuck to each one that read "From the kitchen of," and then Lila's handwritten name. They were arranged by fruit: blackberry, strawberry, pear, peach, apple, orange. Mira took a jar of the peach.

Lila did a weird flash of her eyes toward the ceiling, then said too quickly, "I'm going to ask you something I don't have a right to ask." Lila cupped her hand around her chin. "Did my name ever come up?"

Mira lowered her eyes, aimed them on Lila's neck, her tiny Adam's apple, the size of an orange seed, the sunken round pit in the middle of her collarbone, the chords that stemmed from her neck down into her shoulders, like roots from a tree trunk. "It never did," Mira answered.

Before Mira left, Lila asked if she had any more questions, which Mira thought was one of the odder things she could have said. "Thanks for the marmalade" was the only answer she could think of.

With a finger to one eye, Lila pressed the other against the peephole and watched Mira go down the steps. She tried to detect some hint of Wesley's walk but could not.

She went to the kitchen, took a Valium, then filled a pitcher with water for sun tea. She grabbed some tea bags, went to the backyard, and sat down in one of the chairs at the wrought-iron table, which was cupped by a semicircle of crepe myrtles, their blooms as pink as bubble gum. She dipped the bags into the pitcher a few times, then let them float free.

Pretending that Wesley's eyes were on her, Lila sat in the most flattering way, leaned back, hair hanging down behind her, legs crossed and tilted to the side in the way that Wesley had said made her look like Lauren Bacall—his other secret flame, he had once told her.

Her eyes floated to the pitcher where the tea had marbleized into the water, then clouded up. She tilted her head farther back and looked up and around for what Wesley had always called the "day moon." After a few squinting seconds, she spotted it, a perfect circle high and alone in the sky.

Driving back to the motel, Mira tried to picture Wesley with Lila. All Mira could come up with was a blurry image of the two of them, giddy from the tea's caffeine, picking each other's brains for bits of crossword trivia, laughing at each other's malapropisms, knowing that all of it was part of an illicit act, consummated or not.

Her hands smelled of oranges for the rest of the night, and she wondered if a motel maid would be insulted if her tip came in marmalade form.

On a grassy acre behind the Ona Island BPOE lodge, Kat sat eating coleslaw and oblong corn-bread sticks while the rest waited in line for their pick of the pig. Though the thing's limbs were stiffened and its skin was barely skin anymore, just a reddish brown crisp, its body, head and all, was still intact, its eyes too open for it to look anything other than alive. Kat lasted halfway through the line before opting instead for the side-dish station.

She figured there were about fifty people at the pig picking but decided it felt like more because they all seemed oversized, as if it were a Big and Tall convention. They were loud to match. The kegs had arrived with the pig at dawn, and the drunkenness, along with the heat and humidity, gave everyone a flushed, giddy look, as if they were all in their eighth month of pregnancy.

Kat spotted Aron walking toward her. He was leading by the elbow a tall guy who was scarecrow-skinny and smiled with squinting eyes, as if he was trying to read something that was just out of sight.

The two came up and each propped a leg on the bench where Kat was sitting cross-legged. "Meet an old flame of Mira's." Aron moved his cup in the guy's direction, sloshing him a little. "I told him we were moving a house for the DeLands."

"Ben Hoppert," the guy said with a saucy smile.

"I'm the little sister." Aron walked back toward the pit.

"You don't favor her."

"Her loss," Kat responded, not really meaning it. "So you knew her?"

"I was only in love with her K through five. I never actually told her so to her face, even though I practiced a thousand times. 'You smell like a spring bud. I see your shape in the clouds and the wind and the water. Will you go with me?' "

"I like the second one."

He seemed to take this absolutely seriously. "Thank you. Do you think she would have said yes?" But an instant after he said it, he held his hand up. "No, don't answer that. I can't deal with regret."

"Then she would've told my mom to beat the hell out of you."

"I feel better. I'm married now anyway." He smoothed a quick hand across his stubble as if only now realizing he had forgotten to shave. "So what does she do now?"

"She teaches city planning. Very dull stuff."

"Tell her I'm a pro bono lawyer."

"What do you really do?"

"Contract work."

"*No comprendo.*"

"I'm an electrician."

"I'll tell her you work for the poor."

"And the disabled." He smiled, then looked over his shoulder toward the pit. "I'm gonna see if they've gotten to the white meat."

"Nice meeting you."

"Yeah. Tell Mira what I told you about that cloud thing."

Kat rolled her eyes for lack of a clever thing to say. Ben Hoppert seemed to notice. "Or just tell her I said hello."

Kat spotted Felissa heading toward her, heavy-duty paper plate loaded. Ray had gotten cornered by one of the crewmen from earlier and was eating as they talked. Aron had staked out the beer station.

Felissa sat down and nodded toward Aron. "Ar Bear's trying to find out what BPOE stands for." She sat too close to Kat on the bench and oversmiled at her.

"What?" Kat asked, spotting a fleck of pork wedged between Felissa's two front teeth.

"Do me a big, big, big girl favor."

"What's a girl favor?" Kat lifted her thighs and scratched at the imprints left there by the bench's planks.

"This doesn't even really count as a favor because all it is is you call my mom and dad and ask about me and see what their take is. Tell them you're Becca Dalby from Stephen Foster Elementary, remind them how you moved away to Virginia ten years ago, and say you just wanted to track me down. If they ask how your mother is, just tell them she's on conditional release and getting along swimmingly with her parole officer."

"You're a sicko. There's no phone, anyway."

"Ray's got a cell. It'll take ten secs. You'll call up, ask if I'm there. Dad'll say no, you'll ask where I went, Dad'll go, 'Oh, she went up to No Good for the week,' and you'll hear my Mom cooing in the background. You'll go, 'Thanks for the info,' and they'll get back to watching *Prime Time Justice* and you'll be off the hook."

"Court TV is evil."

"So you're a meat *and* TV snob."

"Now half the country's courtroom sketch artists are like 'That'll be ninety-nine cents. Please drive around.' "

"Don't knock the food-service industry. I happen to believe it's a noble career path, not unlike cosmetology. You satisfy a basic need, build up a clientele, live on tips, and have to keep your fingernails clean." Felissa tried to cut into her pork thigh and broke a prong. "I did my stint as a waitress but got fired because this guy told me to fish the carrot medallions out of his salsa and I told him that wasn't part of my job description. Turns out he was some commissioner of something, so I got the boot. It was for the better, though. The hair net got to me. Vanity, I'll admit to."

Kat raised her eyebrows at Felissa. "What about Ar Bear's little display at the truck stop?"

"About the buffet being closed?"

"FYI, Aron got us kicked out."

Felissa waved her saucy fingers in Kat's face, urging the story on. Kat described what had happened with Vanda, enjoying the brief power trip as Felissa's eyes widened and she chewed in slow motion. Afterward, Felissa offered a stern thank-you and said she would follow up on it. Then she went back to the phone call.

"Come on. I'll do you a big favor."

"Like what?"

"Double-pierce your ears."

"How about don't tell Mira I did this?"

"Deal," Felissa said.

A few minutes later, Felissa mouthed cues as Kat made the call on Ray's cell phone between two parked 4 × 4s, away from the noise. Felissa's father answered. After some frenzied whispering away from the phone, he told Becca Dalby that Felissa had been missing for a week and he was surprised she hadn't seen the spots on the news, that Virginia stations had picked the story up the day before.

Off the phone, Kat told Felissa what her father had said. Felissa did her laugh with no smile and said he had always been prone to overreaction.

Mira was in bed when the rest got back from the pig picking. Ray called after he got to his room to let her know about the plan for tomorrow.

"Okay, let's hear it."

"I think we should leave about eight."

"That's quite the elaborate plan."

"Yeah, I got a flair for plans." There was a pause. Mira wasn't sure where Aron and Felissa were but figured from what Ray said next that they weren't within earshot. "Actually, the plan was to say I missed you tonight."

It was that there was no precedent for this, that it was not something that he needed to say, that it was even on the verge of being inappropriate that made Mira feel as if Ray could do anything to her at that point. She would be fine, as long as he did something.

 *Ten*

There's a paradox to interstate travel. You've never been to the rest stops, you've never seen the people, but somehow they all look familiar. The exits stem from the highway like streams from a river you've been down a thousand times. The alien roadside towns seem to have no life other than the life you give them when you stop at their food, gas, and lodging establishments. When you leave, you assume they shrivel back up into lifeless dots on a road map. The people seem planted like props, barely living things, as if they exist only to make the place feel lifelike while you're there, just for your sake. It all feels cut out of the same mold, but the way it ends up, this sameness only reinforces the fact that you're nowhere near home.

The transient feel of the interstate was working on Mira as she drove. At first, she was determined for Kat not to notice. She tried to make conversation, which came out vapid. She asked about the pig picking; Kat said it bothered her more than she thought it might. Mira asked whether Kat had met anyone, whether she remembered any names. Without hesitation, Kat shook her head. Mira muttered something about the way the house blew waves of air into the median's wildflowers, all green and purple, part of a Tennessee wildflower program, and Kat said she wondered if they were still considered wild if the state planted them. Mira laughed, but it came out fake, as if she had been prompted by a cue card.

She wanted to talk about anything besides Lila, but Kat wouldn't let her get away with this. "So are you gonna tell me what happened last night?" she asked.

"No big revelations," Mira said. "Dad built her house."

"What else?"

"She says they didn't have an affair," though even as Mira said it, she knew they couldn't be certain, and she wasn't sure it mattered whether they had or not.

"So we're moving a house named either for Dad's close friend or his mistress?"

"I guess we are," Mira answered.

A couple passed on a luxury motorcycle, a Goldwing, Mira thought. They were talking back and forth into microphones that curved around to just in front of their lips. They wore the garb: matching leather jackets and cruising pants with fringe down the side, black roper boots, sterling silver rings with turquoise faces the size of quarters. They acknowledged Mira with a bob of their black metallic helmets, which stayed aimed at the house as they passed, as if they were filing away details to fuel their description of it later.

Then Kat said, "He betrayed Mom." Her knees were twitching up and down, propelled by her toes, like an engine's pistons.

Mira replayed her father's last admonitions, his pleas to forget certain things that had happened, to be selective about what she told Kat. This was to the crackle of the CB, the drone of eastbound and westbound engines in different pitches, and the grainy whir of the tires against the asphalt. It was only then, amid this highway clatter, that Mira let herself imagine her father trying to conceal his own secret as much as her mother's. It was Lila, whatever she had been to him, that he feared would be discovered, along with other things. He had gotten caught.

Mira could picture a Saturday morning in the Scamp with her father. They had been on the way to the feed store for mulch, and she had found a packed lunch—tuna on white bread, soggy and gray—wedged underneath the seat. It hadn't hit her as incriminating right away, just a little odd. But when Wesley saw her with it, he fumbled around about how he had a stomach bug and no appetite, which Mira knew wasn't quite right, because the night before he had eaten so much ham loaf with such ferocity that her mother had asked if he didn't just want her to liquefy it so he could get it down faster. Even though Mira had been suspicious of his stomach bug story, she figured at worst he was guilty of sneaking fast food, or not liking his wife's tuna salad.

Mira thought about how familiar Lila's house was, like a toy boxed up for twenty years, then rediscovered. She wondered if they had made frequent drive-bys, maybe under the guise of seeing how the roof tiles were holding up, though in the next instant, Mira acknowledged that she had been guilty of the same thing in relationships, some low-grade form of stalking. And the name. The family line had always been that no one remembered where the name Lila came from, but that seemed now to be one of those tiny myths, along with some that aren't so tiny, that families create and perpetuate until they become part of the folklore.

Mira vaguely remembered the crossword phase he had gone through. It had come out of nowhere. She could still see her mother ridiculing him, telling him to get a man's hobby already, which just made him more fanatic about the puzzles, increased their appeal. And thinking about it now, Mira didn't blame him for that.

Then Kat said again, "He betrayed her's what I think."

Mira's focus ricocheted from one image to another, like out-of-sequence animation, and she knew that whatever frame it ended up on would determine what she said next. First Eve's idealized heirloom portrait of the house, then the elegant woman for whom the house had been named, then the almost gruesome elongation of Wesley's neck in its sling. Last was Reverend Joseph Bleecher's smiling, fleshy face as Helen seductively cut his hair on the front porch, Mira's own numb eyes pointed their way, Kearney cluelessly scooping up the wiry gray locks to glue to his collage on the house's side.

"Mom's no angel in this." Mira was certain when she said it—and once she saw the look on Kat's face of immediate understanding at what she might be getting at—how the rest of the hours in the pickup that day would be spent. She knew also, maybe melodramatically, that this would be one of those moments that's etched on you like a brand, or a scar, but one that some good might come from nonetheless.

For eleven years, the DeLands had attended Success Baptist Church on Easter, Christmas, and other days when their absence would be noticed. "Never religiously," Mira had once heard her father say. Its members—the Successors, they liked to be called—seemed to be in a constant state of congratulating themselves for belonging to the oldest church in the county. Its deacons were the descendants of the town's founders as well as the church's, and for the good fortune and reputation they brought to Success, their names were inscribed inside leather-bound hymnals and engraved on gold plates glued to the ends of wooden pews. The DeLands not being a part of this tradition—they had chosen Success from the Yellow

Pages—Mira always felt like a provisional member. They all felt it; they were the church's riffraff.

And on days that they attended, reminders of this were everywhere. First, there would be the dilemma of pew selection. Weekly churchgoers had long ago staked out pews for themselves. But the DeLands never went enough Sundays in a row for this to apply to them. So rather than risk offending the system, the four of them would hover with the smokers just outside the double doors until the choir started its prelude. Only then would they slink into the sanctuary and scan for a free pew.

Even worse for Mira had been the trauma of the collection plate. Firmly entrenched members would deposit envelopes she didn't recognize, as if there were a special method of payment reserved for those who dutifully gave alms. For the DeLands' part, Wesley would lay a soiled dollar in the plate, and Kearney and Mira would each deposit a quarter that their mother had given them before church. Mira would try to land the quarter on a bill or envelope, but more than not fail at this and cower mortified as the coin rang against the stainless steel.

Even their exit from the sanctuary would have given a clue to anyone who was paying attention that the DeLands weren't insiders. As soon as the choir started the processional, the congregation would file into the center aisle to head out through the double doors. Reverend Bleecher, still flushed and drunklike from the sermon, would greet them as they left. He would cup the hand each extended toward him in both of his, giving it two shakes, as if he were rolling dice. Just outside the church, instead of a mad rush for the parking lot, the newly revived would loiter like it was intermission, compliment the sermon, discuss the status of the prayer circles, all the time fanning themselves with their bulletins, which they would be sure to hang on to for a discount at most any Sunday lunch buffet. As for the DeLands, they would exit through a side door and be halfway to Bonanza before the last Successor made his way out of the sanctuary.

Mira always suspected that this feeling of being transient members added to her mother's satisfaction when she was lured into bed by Reverend Bleecher. The idea wasn't lost on Mira, even at age ten, that a such a man might use his position to entice women. But all the signs were that Reverend Bleecher's seduction of her mother had been a secular one, carried out with the same flatteries and charms that a layman would use.

These signs came straight from her mother, who began early in the relationship to speak of it casually at dinner or over lulls in television, as if it were a natural topic of conversation. She first broke the news on a Saturday morning over French toast, which Mira hadn't eaten since.

"I'll be away this afternoon," she said, spiraling syrup onto her plate. "I'm going fishing with Reverend Bleecher." Mira's father's eyes shot toward her, waiting for an explanation, or a laugh, but neither came.

"What's the occasion?" he asked in his calm way.

"We've discovered that fishing is a common interest." She poked a mocking finger into her cheek. "Is that an occasion?"

Their father waved for Kearney and Mira to take their plates outside, as if the usual seclusion of the bedroom wouldn't suffice this time. They had just finished their French toast a few minutes later when he came out and sat between them on the steps.

"I don't want you kids to give another thought to what just happened in there." And that was it. The tone was set for the next year of their mother's early exits from meals, the torture of weekly church attendance, and unabashed banter about the virtues of Reverend Bleecher. His visits to the house always came when their father wasn't there, not because she timed them so, but because Wesley always knew beforehand and planned to be away from the house. Why he didn't make a habit of taking her and Kearney with him, Mira never figured out.

On days when Reverend Bleecher came over, he and Helen would sit in rocking chairs on the porch and drink scalding coffee. "It's gotta make your tongue sweat," Mira had once heard him say before sending her mother back in for a hotter cup. They would mull over church gossip, tell insider Baptist jokes, glow over their kids' milestones—his son's victory at the academic Olympics, his daughter's first speeding ticket, Mira's premature first period, Kearney's selection as first-chair clarinet—as if the children were the product of their own relationship.

One Saturday, Reverend Bleecher drove up with a dozen fishing rods poking out of the side window of his Cutlass Supreme. He was a passionate fisherman—prayed for fish and fished for God, he said—and wanted to work on Helen's cast before their next excursion. Using the picnic table in the backyard as a pier, Reverend Bleecher started with a demonstration, casting into the grass, then pretending to have a bite, bending backward, feigning a look of strain until his face turned red. Helen stood on the other end of the table, laughing uncontrollably, waving her hand in front of her face. Then it was her turn. Reverend Bleecher stood behind her, guiding her arms as she cast, first with no line attached, then with the line so she could get the feel of it. After a dozen practice casts, Reverend Bleecher got off the table and watched as she tried each of the rods, looking for the best fit, as if sizing a golf club, as if it really mattered. The next Saturday, Reverend Bleecher dropped her off after an outing to Lake Newman. She walked in the front door, red-faced from sun and giddiness over the cleaned sturgeon she had brought home to fry.

It was during a visit soon after that that Mira found them in the kitchen. She had been drawing on the side of the house but figured the coast would be clear, since they knew she was around. When she walked in the front door, there were no voices, just the rush of running water, which she followed to the kitchen. There, Helen was sitting on a stool, her back to the sink, neck arced so that her head hung under the faucet. Reverend Bleecher stood over her, his body leaning into her side, hands entangled in the lather of her hair, massaging her scalp. Helen's eyes were closed, and she was smiling a little, luxuriating, saying things Mira couldn't hear over the water. As she looked on, Mira imagined Reverend Bleecher dipping adolescents into the baptistery, reciting the appropriate blessings, then raising from the water the newly baptized, who were disoriented and soaking wet. Mira walked back outside, unsure of whether she had gone unseen or just been ignored.

It was a few weeks after that, on a Monday, that a stomach virus kept her home from school. When Reverend Bleecher came over midmorning, it didn't occur to her that they might have planned something for when she wouldn't be home, that she was cramping her own mother's style. The two of them had been on the front porch for an hour when Helen came in and asked how she was feeling, and when Mira said she was better, Helen suggested that she walk the half a mile to the Piggly Wiggly to get some milk. It was a hot day, so Mira whined and only agreed to go after Reverend Bleecher said he would chip in for a candy bar. She was a few blocks away, half-thinking about how much he reminded her of the actor Vic Tayback, when she realized in a nauseous instant that she had been wrong about feeling better. Before she could make a run for the house, she threw up between a cluster of anthills on the side of the road and decided from the way they scurried toward the puddle that she had done them a favor. Mira gave up on the milk, and in a few minutes, when she got back to the house, she heard the heavy breathing and squeaking of the bedsprings, which were her only associations with sex. Even after she had come in the front door and closed it behind her, when they must have known someone was there, the noises didn't stop. No one called out to see who it was. Mira walked to the bedroom door as quietly as a body could. It was closed, but there was just enough of a crack in the middle—it was a combination door—for Mira to see the lumps of Helen and Reverend Bleecher writhing under the covers.

Even then, when she had only a vague idea of what they might be up to, Mira was embarrassed for her more than anything. In those days, she began to think of her mother as one of those streakers of the late seventies, shameless, throwing their nakedness at captive crowds and television audiences, thrilled by the number of people they could offend with a single disrobing.

Then one July night at dinner, a few months after the bedroom scene, her mother shared some fresh gossip about the Mortmans—he a deacon, she the choir director at church. Helen had just heard that they were having marital problems because of his sterility, and Reverend Bleecher had been serving as their marriage counselor. It took another six months for her mother to find out from an inside source that Reverend Bleecher had also been serving as the Mortmans' infertility counselor and was kindly supplying Mrs. Mortman with some seed of his own. As casually as she had the initial news of her affair, Helen shared the latest with the family, this time over salmon croquettes.

"He says I was like a prescription drug. First he used me for medicinal purposes." Her face seemed to contract, every muscle tensing up. She was squeezing the words out like water from a wet rag. "Then for recreation. Now he's over me, like a blasted drug he's used so much that it doesn't work on him anymore."

More than anything, Mira could remember the spectacle of her father getting up from his chair and standing behind Helen, bending down so that his arms cradled her head. As she wailed, he kissed her hair and massaged her shoulders in small circles, whispering over and over, "Okay, love, it's okay, love."

The next day, Helen woke up determined to move west of the Mississippi. She would go anywhere, just get her west of the Mississippi. It was when Wesley got a job managing a contracting company in Mims that they decided on Arkansas. Most of the plans were made behind closed doors—Mira thought the sudden secrecy was odd—but it became clear enough that Wesley had argued hard for the family to stay put. In the end, they agreed to move but not to sell the house, a decision they could afford to make because, in addition to having a good job waiting for him, Wesley had just gotten a manufacturer for his water-sensitive windshield wipers, self-adjusting, depending on how much rain fell. Keeping the house, not selling it off, was their mother's concession to him, one of few. Wesley's concession was the move to Arkansas itself, though this was not difficult for him to make; he viewed it as a marriage-saving one.

Soon after the move, once Mira was settled into sixth grade and Kearney into ninth, their father suggested they join another church, for the kids' sake, if nothing else. Despite his wife's emphatic no, he started bringing home literature on the area's churches from the Chamber of Commerce, slipping it into her *Ladies' Home Journal.*

Thinking maybe she would be open to a different denomination, he brought home Methodist and Presbyterian bulletins along with the Baptist, and without fail, he would find them trashed a day later. One Sunday morning, they were all in the living room and he switched the TV to a church service. Before Helen could make Wesley change the channel, a passage from Philippians appeared on the screen, and Kearney asked if that's where their Uncle Earl had been stationed. Wesley looked at Helen and said, "See?"

"Yes, sweet potato, it is," Helen had said before switching the TV back to the dog show they had been watching.

Helen wouldn't be swayed. Religion in all forms was suddenly nonsense in her eyes, "unutterable vileness of the most dangerous kind," she would sometimes quote Lenin as having said, leaving them to wonder where she had picked this bit up. She developed the knack of using religion as an excuse not to take certain people seriously, as a decider of who was worthy of the school board or city council, as a personality test of who was rational and who was a flake.

It was as if a glaze had been painted over the details of their lives in the old house. They became untouchable things from the past, like antique figurines so fragile, they're not to be toyed with. Helen reasoned that once Kat was born, a year and a half after the move, there was an even greater need to leave Ona Island behind, and she saw to it that everyone developed a selectively fuzzy memory about life prior to the Reagan-Bush era. The only time Helen ever slapped Mira on the face was when Mira was fifteen and pointed out an uncomfortable irony: that the ugliness that her mother had been so blatant about with the rest of them while it was going on, she was now conspiring to hide from Kat as if all good depended on it.

———

Afterward, through thirty mile markers, Kat refused eye contact, so Mira's stare floated from the road to the cruel joke of the house's back door, hanging five feet over nothing but the asphalt flying by below. Back to the road, then to a flock of small black birds flying north in a perfect V formation, like the Blue Angels. A glance at the road as they were passed by a semi, then the fleeting view off to the right, all faded billboards and endless acres of fenced countryside.

They passed a billboard for Trucker's Oasis, this one with a three-dimensional cutout of Dewight's head waving in the corner. Twenty miles later, they made a quick stop at Trucker's Oasis, just long enough for Aron to make his amends with Vanda, Ray said over the CB. Felissa and Aron went inside while the rest waited in the trucks. Five minutes later, they came out with linked hands, and the look on Felissa's face made Mira think that Vanda had been in a forgiving mood.

Through all of this, Kat said nothing, sitting erect, a hand cupped under each thigh. She seemed so distant that when she finally spoke up, it blew Mira away.

"She must've known about Lila," Kat blurted out. "That must be why she did it, and flaunted it that way." Her voice was unflinching. Whether she really believed what she was saying, or was just trying to convince herself of it, Mira wasn't sure. But Mira could feel herself not buying Kat's generous take on things.

"Maybe" was all Mira could think of to say.

"So why did you tell me this?"

Mira played with the adjustment of the rearview mirror, which was fine in the first place, just to buy a minute, then said, "You and all your 'I'm a grown-up' talk lately."

"This isn't what I thought it would get me." Kat looked down toward her lap and started combing her fingers through the unraveled threads of her cutoffs.

"Plus," Mira added, "I figured it was a big thing to let slide, like before."

Plotting sarcasm, Kat cocked her head, set her mouth to speak, and then after an effective delay of a few seconds, she said, "And this is the same affair that Mom tried to protect me from by destroying every photo of the house within her reach, right?"

Mira didn't know what to say, so she kept quiet, focused her eyes on the house ahead of them, the way some of the wood planks were warped and loose roof tiles flapped in the wind, the reflection of the revolving orange lights in the trembling back door window.

Kat went on, "And the same one that Dad tried to protect me from by moving the house, right?" She was having to force the words out, her voice getting croaky. Her eyes pooled with tears, about to overflow.

Mira opened her mouth to defend herself, then balked and said nothing. There was no good thing to say. Kat knew the answers to her own questions. It wasn't like she had misunderstood, like it had really been someone else's mother, not theirs, or like Mira had let it slip out by accident. Mira had known what she was doing, and Kat had understood every word, so Mira just sat there feeling cruel, not because she had taken any pleasure in hurting her, but because all she could do was avoid Kat's stare.

Within a minute, Kat was crying, not a whiny cry, but the kind that doubles you over, the kind where you can't see for the tears and squinting eyes, and you forget to breathe.

It was when Mira tried to reach for her hand—Kat dodged it— that she felt the road roughen, and Kat yelled something Mira couldn't understand as she looked up and found them straddling the right lane and shoulder. Mira jerked the wheel back toward the center but overcompensated, veering halfway into the left lane. Only after she had steered them back did she look over her shoulder and see that no cars had been anywhere near them. Mira felt the light-headed weariness of an adrenaline rush subsiding. The static of Ray's voice came in over the CB.

"This's Big Rig. What was that? Over."

Mira picked up the microphone. "Sorry."

"We'll stop at the first motel that's got the space for us," Ray told them. "Aron says it can't be a Holiday Inn Express. Over and out."

The discussion dead, they sat there recovering. The scare had stopped Kat's crying. Mira shifted her eyes between the sky and the interstate, which seemed to liquefy off in the distance. The sun had dodged the transparent clouds all afternoon, leaving them squinting to the west as they drove in what felt like slow motion, cars blowing past at twice their speed. The heat of earlier had softened to a sleep-inducing warmth.

They passed a cleanup crew in the median, a dozen guys Kat's age, each with a crew cut and orange vest, a garbage bag in one hand, a poker in the other. They stopped what they were doing to look at Mira as she drove by, not the truck or the house ahead, but Mira, desperate for anything, but eye contact would do.

Eleven

The motel they stayed at was locally owned, a bland thing in over its head in tackiness: narrow beds sunken in the middle, dark orange carpet stained from use and spills, a green Bible the size of an index card, everything bolted down, a too-small bedspread that revealed the always disappointing wooden pedestal supporting the mattress. An owl painting hung over each bed, the direction of the owl's stare the only difference between the two. The room smelled of air freshener, meant to disguise the collective smells of all the previous guests.

Just as she and Mira got inside, Kat turned on the TV—as much an instinct for her as turning on the light—which was screwed into a shelf that pointed down at an angle from the wall. Mira scanned the phone book for DeLands, a habit she had gotten from her father. There were none.

Mira lay down and decided to feign sleep, anything to lessen the awkwardness of Kat pretending she was alone. The room was dark except for the TV and columns of late-afternoon light let in from the sides of the rubberized curtains, which were too small for the window. More tired than she realized, Mira was in a nitrous oxide–like sleep after a few minutes, fading in and out, minutes like seconds, no more disturbed by the TV six feet away than she would have been by the tinkling of metal tools and the murmur of dentist and hygienist. She glanced Kat's way a couple of times in between waves. The whites of her eyes shined in the TV's powdery light.

As they left to find a place to eat dinner, Mira asked the clerk at the front desk for a recommendation. She was a tall, thick-boned woman with gorgeous big eyes to match, though one was noticeably higher than the other. She said she would place her bets on Rod's Chinese House and gave Mira directions. Aron insisted they all go the few miles in his truck, so Felissa jumped into the bed, and when no one else volunteered, Ray said he would join her.

Halfway there, when there was no oncoming traffic, Aron serpentined across the two lanes, his eyes locked on the rearview mirror. Ray was leaning against one wheel well with his boots up against the other. He was looking Aron's way, his lips mouthing insults, the sound getting lost in the whip of the wind. Felissa was lying down, undisturbed, eyes fixed on the sky.

Rod's Chinese House seemed to have been a steak house in its former life. The Old West decor—a mounted deer head, saloon doors, wagon wheels converted to light fixtures—remained but now took on a hint of East Asia: Chinese paper lanterns giving off opaque light and a kimono splayed across a wall. They all got the buffet and iced tea. Mira added a vodka tonic to her order.

"So what's your issue with Holiday Inn Express?" Mira asked Aron. They were in the buffet line, talking into the plastic cough guard. Kat and Felissa were lagging behind.

"He had a bad hair experience last night," Ray explained, standing just in front of Aron.

"Okay, help us settle this," Aron said to Mira. "You think they change both beds if it looks like only one's been slept in?"

"I thought it was a law or something." Mira figured her answer came down on Ray's side. He looked at Aron as if his point had been made.

"What if just the pillows were used," Aron went on, "like if somebody wanted all four on one bed?"

Mira nudged him to move down. They were holding up the line. "That's where the maid's judgment comes into play."

"All I know is, I found more than one hair when I turned down the bed last night." Aron tapped the air with the chicken-wing tongs.

"Probably got mixed in with the laundry," Mira replied, "all those stray fibers swishing around in there."

"I should do one of those exposés," Aron said. They were heading back to the table. "I could stay in a double room one night, plant a few hairs on the bed I didn't sleep in, but leave it all made up and smooth. Then I could get someone else to stay there the next night and see if the sheets had been changed."

"Or you could use a hidden camera." Mira took a seat next to Ray.

As if he hadn't heard her, Aron went on: "Fact, I could do it at every major chain, and some independents for balance."

Ray spun a small carousel of sauces. "That would rock the motel world."

"You could take it to the Better Business Bureau," Mira said.

Aron sputtered his lips. "Small beans. I'd go to *Geraldo*."

Felissa arrived from the buffet. "Let me guess. He's on the hair again."

"I think you mean potatoes," Mira said Aron's way. Kat took a seat next to Ray.

A pretty waitress leaned down to their eye level. "Y'all's drinks okay?" She spoke with a sweet twang. Her red hair was twisted into perfect tight curls, each one like a phone cord. Aron asked for some coffee.

"So tell the people what you're gonna do for me, Ar." Felissa combed her nails through Aron's platinum hair.

"I'm not doing it, sweet thing."

"Doing what?" Ray asked.

"Aron here is going to give the authorities a call and tell them he's a truck driver and he saw someone fitting my description, although much prettier, at a BP in Kentucky, so he was just being a good Christian and reporting it." As she spoke, she looked at Aron with raised eyebrows—plucked to sideways commas—as if this was another rehearsal of the plan.

Aron made a smacking sound with his mouth. "Yeah, then they'll ask what trucking company I work for, I'll make one up, they'll call it up for verification and some granny in pink rollers'll answer, and they'll know I'm a fraud."

Mira flashed a squint at Felissa. "You're missing?" Kat was busy studying the contents of her egg roll.

"I'm eighteen and it's a free country." Felissa looked back at Aron. "Fine, say you're a tourist from Canada—no, Australia—and you're leaving tomorrow. They're not gonna go calling overseas to check on you. You can use your British accent. Same as the Australian."

Ray rested his forehead on a thumb. "This was not in the itinerary."

"Oh, don't get all good on me. Look, it would only be cruel if I wasn't okay, but I'm okay, see? Safe and sound. Clothed and fed.

In good hands. Aron won't even be saying otherwise. He's just saying he saw me where he didn't. I can think of worse things. You know what happened the last time I went AWOL? It was the day before my parents left for vacation and I tried to be nice and leave a note of explanation, but they pretended not to see it so that they could still go to Opryland, acted all freaked-out when they got back, like they'd just discovered it."

Mira forced a smile and said, "Or else you're just saying that."

"Aron believes me." Felissa kissed his temple. "That will suffice."

Kat had barely said a word since they had left the motel, so they were all surprised when she broke in. "So, Ray, how many houses have you moved?"

He was working on his egg-drop soup. "One hundred and eighty, matter of fact."

"Aron?"

"In the dozens, I 'magine."

"So, generally, why do people move houses?" she asked. "The most common reasons, I mean."

"Easy," Aron said. "The house is sold to a new owner who wants to put it on his land."

Aron was the only one to use the chopsticks, and he did so with the grace and coordination of someone who had never seen a metal utensil. He must have caught Mira looking impressed. "Savoir faire," he muttered without trying to pull off a French accent.

"Okay, other than that, what are some reasons?" Though Kat wouldn't look at her, Mira knew the display was for her benefit. She wondered if anyone could detect her eyelid twitching.

Ray and Aron set their food aside and looked at each other as they brainstormed—Ray leaning back in his chair, arms folded across his chest, Aron bending forward, elbows on the table, one hand picking at the centerpiece, a wine bottle turned candle holder, so waxed over in reds and greens and whites that the glass was nearly invisible. They seemed to want to do justice to the question, as if they appreciated Kat's interest in their trade. It was like a think tank, but on a smaller scale.

"You'll see eminent domain," Ray said. "Sometimes the city'll buy the land right out from under a house. Not much choice in that case."

Felissa dipped the tip of an egg roll into the hot mustard. "There was that one on top of an Indian burial ground in *Poltergeist.*"

"They didn't move the house, dipstick," Aron told her. "I once moved one that turned out to be too close to a chemical plant. No one had caught it before the thing was built."

"Moved several that were in floodplains," Ray said. "Owners couldn't get insurance."

Kat nodded emphatically. "All of which make sense, huh?"

The waitress brought Aron's coffee and, instead of interrupting, lifted her eyebrows to see if they wanted anything else. Mira ticked a fingernail against her almost-empty glass.

"Always thought so at the time." Ray wondered about her point.

"Okay," Kat said. "How about so that a dead adulterous husband can spite a dead adulterous wife?" Ray and Aron backed away from this, keeping quiet, as if they had walked in on something they knew they weren't meant to see.

As for Mira, she dropped her fork louder than she had meant to against her plate and sunk her face into her hands, which smelled of egg rolls. "That's helpful."

Kat rejoined her fried rice. "I'm glad."

———

For the drive back to the motel, Kat crawled into the bed of the pickup before anyone could argue with her. Felissa followed her. Mira sat between Aron and Ray in the cab.

"Anybody want to catch a flick tonight?" Aron asked. They had passed a small theater on the way into town, two screens at the most, all shows a dollar. But before they had a chance to answer, Aron slammed his fist into the steering wheel. "They didn't give us our fortune cookies."

"That's bad luck," Mira said, though she had never heard this.

Ray winked at her and put on an exaggerated look of optimism. "We're gonna have so much good luck, we're gonna need the bad to keep tabs on the good."

"Okay, Mister Rogers," Mira said, playing along.

"So was Kat's bit for real?" Aron twitched his head toward the back.

"Not completely." Mira looked away, hoping he would let it go at that. "Was Felissa's?"

"No way." He paused to dig at a molar with his toothpick. "She's prepping for a guest spot on *Jenny Jones*."

Driving back to the motel, the faded town hit Mira differently from the way it had in the daylight. The darkness served it well, the way it threw the blandness into shadow. All that was left were signs in primary colors, lit up in neon and fluorescent. She tried squinting, and it became a Lite Brite skyline.

Mira swiveled around to look in the truckbed. Felissa was lying down again, this time busy pushing her nail cuticles back. Kat sat cross-legged, facing the cab. The moon was almost full, like a child-drawn circle, not quite perfect. Kat looked beautiful in its milky light, her eyes closed, hair whipping horizontally behind her, as if she was in a wind tunnel.

Back at the motel, Kat and Mira had been locked in the room for almost an hour when Mira decided to call Ray. She dialed the wrong room number and got a little kid on the other end. On the second dial, Ray answered.

"Can I come over for a while?" she asked into the phone, glancing at Kat, whose eyes were locked onto the TV. She was averaging about three seconds per channel.

"Now?"

"It's only the shank of the evening," Mira said. She could hear water running in the background. "I'll bring my thermos."

"I s'pose that would be nice."

Mira hung up and looked at Kat, who still refused even to glance her way. "Mind if I go visit with Ray?"

Kat switched the remote to her fresh hand. "Knock yourself up."

"There's Miss Vodka Tonic." Ray had left the door cracked. He was opening the dresser drawers, bending to see if they were empty, then closing them. Mira could tell he had just showered: the smell of deodorant soap, the mirror still patched with steam, wide comb marks in his damp hair, his shirt clinging to his back as if he hadn't dried off all the way.

They sat down in the room's only two chairs, vinyl beige things that swiveled and reclined in all directions. His room had a marine motif: two pastel oil paintings of conchs, roundish sand dollars splayed across the bedspread, carpet the color of beach sand, an accidental match.

"So where's Captain and Tenille?" Mira asked.

"They went to see some Steven Seagal thing. They had to find a phone booth first."

"You've got a phone."

"Aron did it on condition of complete anonymity." Ray peeled the wrap off of two plastic cups—the small, flimsy kind that Mira associated with urine specimens—and poured muscadine wine from the thermos into each one. Then Mira held her cup up between them. "A toast."

"To what?" Ray swirled the wine in tiny circles.

"That was your cue. Man makes toast."

Ray smiled. His teeth were completely straight except for one on the top right side, perfectly askew, turned at an angle so that it overlapped just slightly with the next tooth.

"To lounging in chanky motels," he said. The cups tapped almost inaudibly as they met across the table.

"That was lovely."

Ray patted himself on the chest. "I belong to Toastmaster's."

Mira reclined in the chair, nudged her shoes off, and rested her feet on the bed beside her. "So've you talked to Liz?"

"We talk every day."

"That's not very separated."

Ray took a drink for a time-killing pause. "I know."

"I bet you don't get divorced. You don't seem like an ex-husband kind of guy, I'm telling you." And this was true of Ray, though it hadn't occurred to Mira until the instant before she said it.

"Tell me about an ex-husband kind of guy."

"You know, a Monte Carlo, a dinky sales job, karaoke, a beeper in there somewhere."

"That's not very nice."

Mira stared at an inexplicable fleck of glitter on Ray's temple. "You're absolutely the most totally generous person I know," she said. "I'm sorry. I do divorced men a disservice."

"Today, Liz told me she's not attracted to me anymore."

"You're lying."

He revolved several times in his chair, propelling himself with his feet against the floor and air-conditioning unit. "If I were making things up, I'd think of something more flattering than that, like she decided I was too damn good-looking."

"She'd be right about that," Mira said. He stopped himself with his feet, then leaned forward, resting his elbows on the table.

"Don't go and fluster me."

Mira leaned into the table to meet him. "So you're trying out other people?"

"More like just trying out not being together." He was pressing his thumb into the table's puckering veneer.

"Can you try me?" Mira felt swervy from the drinks and watching Ray spin.

"What if I go back to Liz?"

"Then I guess the separation will've worked." She rang her fingernails against the table. "Let's see a picture of her."

Ray cocked his head and paused. "I don't think I have one on me."

"Is she aware of this?" Mira asked. "She should divorce you. And soon. Not walk, but run to the courthouse."

"She may already be there."

"I want to meet her," Mira said. "Tell her to meet us when we deliver the house."

"She'll be working."

"She can't slip away?"

"What reason am I supposed to give her?"

"Cross your fingers and lie. Tell her I'm considering a new garage door for the house."

"The house doesn't have a garage," Ray pointed out.

"Okay, no lie. Tell her you've got a curious friend."

"What's the fascination?" Ray asked. "Curious about what?"

"Don't be modest."

"What do you want to know?"

"Only everything. Your preferences—paper or plastic, smooth or crunchy, pitted or stuffed. You name it."

"You're drunk."

"I prefer light-headed, thank you."

Ray swiveled to get up from his chair. He went into the bathroom and nudged the door closed, but left it cracked, which Mira found oddly flattering.

She crawled from the chair onto the bed, not letting her feet touch the floor, then lay down. To the light trickle that came from the bathroom, Mira made a mental list of the possible reasons for her Ray fixation. Maybe it was some knee-jerk imitation of her parents. Or she was using Ray as filler for Marcus, but in an instant she knew it was safe to rule that out. Maybe she could blame it on being away from her apartment and teaching, the feeling like she was living someone else's life, like nothing really counted. Or she could call it altruism, doing her selfless part to test the strength of a marriage. That it wasn't her own marriage didn't have to matter, she figured. Or maybe it was just Ray, his CB savvy, or his eyes.

Then she settled on the reason she had come over in the first place, that two doors down, remote in hand, Kat was making a masterpiece out of snubbing her, dealing out the blame.

Mira heard the toilet flush, and in a sodden instant, she let herself off the hook, decided that Liz had been right, that you don't have to have a reason for such things.

Ray was still regrouping his jeans when he came out of the bathroom saying, "It's nine. Guess what's on AMC." Mira shrugged from the bed. "*It Happened One Night.*"

"Never saw it."

"You might get to see me cry." He pulled two pillows from Aron's bed. "This'll set him off."

"We'll plant some hairs."

Over the last of the muscadine wine, they watched the movie in Ray's bed, barefooted, on top of the bedspread, a foot of mattress separating them. The reviewers quoted in the introduction weren't lying about the romance. There wasn't a single kiss, but the escalating banter between Claudette Colbert and Clark Gable did the work a screen kiss would've done.

After the movie and a few minutes into another one, Mira turned onto her side, facing Ray, her head propped on her hand. He had been dozing, but the shifting woke him. He cracked his eyes open. They lay there for a minute in the blue light of the television, holding each other's stare.

Then Ray leaned his head up and kissed her, the sweet smell of the wine wafting between their lips. It was a clean, close-lipped kiss, but it lingered long enough to hint at more to come. Mira imagined that their kiss was the token one omitted from the movie and that to an onlooker, the outlines of their faces would be blurred, reced-

ing into the charcoal background, somehow making them look all
the more real.

They were jolted out of this by the slam of a car door just outside
the room, then the wiggle of a key into the doorknob. They both
jerked out of bed as if an electric current had been driven up
through the springs. All in a couple of awkward seconds, Aron
started to back out before he had gotten through the doorway, Ray
fumbled for the light switch above the nightstand, and Mira muttered that she needed to go anyway, feeling for her shoes beside the
bed. Ray waved Aron back in, Felissa straggling behind him, and
Mira said good night as she left and Ray walked her to her room,
two doors down.

There, they leaned against the cool concrete block, listening to
the whir of interstate traffic mixed with the strain of a dozen air-
conditioning units. Ray's lips were level with her forehead, and he
kissed her there. "Sleep tight."

Mira figured every relationship begins with a moment, and beyond that moment, certain things are assumed and expected, like
you've signed a nonretractable contract. She lay in bed thinking
that she and Ray had had their moment, that things would cre-
scendo from there, and that it would be good, however it turned
out. On her way to sleep, she imagined the patterned rise and fall
of Ray's chest pressed against hers, the phantom feel of his heart-
beat, slower and out of sync with her own, but beating hard, as if
trying to catch up.

Twelve

Mira's driving took on a flair of whimsy the next morning. She let her focus float in and out among the road, her headache, and the few hours she had spent with Ray the night before. It had taken several seconds after she woke up for the memory to come. When it had, she had lain there evaluating it, replaying bits of conversation, Aron and Felissa's surprise entry, wondering why she had enjoyed the awkwardness of it.

Now, in the pickup, Mira drove like an elderly driver in unfamiliar territory. As she took the entrance ramp to the interstate, she slowed to school-zone speed, then stopped before looking over her shoulder for approaching traffic. Not until a long, annoyed honk came from behind did it hit her that she was a menace. A mile onto the interstate, they came to a curve in the road and she flicked her turn signal, which stayed on until a big-haired man in the passenger seat of a de Ville pointed toward her headlights. Mira lagged behind Ray, slipping into a daze, lost in some nice intricacy of the night before, then caught herself going twenty-five. Ray piped in over the CB and gently chastised her. "These things don't come with cruise control," he said. "Keep her near forty."

Her college roommate had called this morning-after mixture of giddiness and stupidity a "love hangover." She had usually said it to describe Mira's behavior. Why she had had so few amorous encounters of her own, Mira could never figure out. She had had the natural good looks of a little girl: straight almost-white hair, milky skin that looked like it had never seen a speck of makeup and was better off because of it, an almost boyish body that she never had to work for. She had had the charisma of a young girl, too, some quality Mira couldn't quite put her finger on, maybe because she didn't have it herself. Her roommate had prided herself on her datelessness, though, as if not having any at all was somehow better than giving it a go and flailing. And about that, Mira figured she may have been right.

If Kat picked up on Mira's mood, maybe secretly enjoying her foolish display, she didn't let on, since so far her game plan for the day had been not to acknowledge Mira at all, even for the worthy purpose of mockery. With her headphones hanging upside down, she was listening to the same song over and over every four minutes, rewinding, listening, rewinding.

Within sight but still miles ahead were low bulbous clouds—some gray, some almost navy, laden with water. Gusts of wind tugged at the truck. Mira's grip stiffened on the wheel. Ahead, the flatbed seemed to be swaying side to side, just slightly, under the weight of the house. The storm had been forecast. Ray had said at breakfast that it was the remnant of a tropical storm, one that had created enough of a scare along the Gulf Coast to cause plywood and Sterno shortages and to fill up shelters, but it had petered out at the last minute. As they broke up toward the trucks for the day's drive, Ray had said, "Roads are slickest when the rain first starts."

Kat's tape player let out a click. She tugged the headphones off with her index finger and muttered something Mira couldn't understand. Then, out of nowhere, she asked, "So how was Ray?" She looked right at Mira for the first time all morning.

"What?" was all Mira could muster.

"What's the story?" Kat fidgeted with a cassette holder: open, close, open, close. "Gimmie the headline."

"There's no story."

"Did he say anything about me?"

"We watched a movie," Mira told her.

"I bet you did."

Mira's window was halfway down, and she thought she smelled rain. Kat's hands were still busy with the tape holder. Kat caught Mira eyeing it, could tell she was annoyed, so she put it right up to Mira's face and snapped it open and shut, open again, then shut it so that it caught the tip of her nose. In a reflex, Mira swatted her away, her hand clapping sharply against Kat's upper arm, like a sound-effect slap in a movie. As some kind of apology, Mira tried to grab for Kat's hand, but Kat pulled away.

"Sorry," Mira said.

"Which subject is it you want to avoid? Ray or sex?"

"You're half-right."

"About which part?" Kat asked.

"Where did sex come in?"

"Which part was I right about?"

"I forget." Mira was staring at the fuzzy remnant of a plane's contrail. The plane was long gone.

"The sex thing?" Kat asked.

"I think so."

"This just off the AP: I may as well have had sex."

"What does that mean?"

"I've done sex."

"Please don't be hurt if I don't pursue that," Mira said.

"I'd be offended if you did," and she started drawing on the rubber sole of her shoe with a ballpoint pen.

Even if they had been in the pattern of telling each other what they were thinking, Mira would've kept what she was thinking then to herself. Part of her wanted to know exactly where and when and with whom it had happened. The rest of her wanted to think about anything else. In some juvenile way, knowing that Kat had come close, that she had gone through this adult thing, in whatever form, changed the way Mira looked at her. It was no different, she guessed, than when she had been in high school and found out the same about a girlfriend. Mira wasn't sure if she was acting her age then or now, or neither.

"This nastiness would be more effective if I knew the exact reason for it," Mira said.

Kat made a smacking noise with her mouth, then held her hand out, counting on her fingers as she spoke: "You ruined the house for me. You did a royal job of screwing Mom up for me. You did what the fuck you wanted to do." Kat let this sit in the air a few seconds, then added, "Pick a reason. I'm having a sale." With this last part, her voice trembled enough to make her look away, which hit Mira as unbearably sad, like catching an illiterate trying to fake reading, or her deaf paternal grandfather pretending to hear, nodding and inserting a yes here and there, when Mira knew all he could make out was a dull buzz. To Mira, at that moment, Kat seemed just barely sixteen.

———

Mira's eyes were fixed on the blur of the asphalt when a flash of something she didn't recognize flew toward the pickup. About the time it slammed into the windshield, she realized it was tire tread. She let out an ugly wail as splinters of glass shot their way and she felt a sharp sting on her right cheek. The windshield was clouded by the shattered glass, so she rolled her window down the rest of the way and leaned out to steer them to the side.

Ray must've felt the tread come loose right away, because he was already coming to a stop well off the shoulder, which happened to be flat.

Mira looked over at Kat, whose hand was pressed flat against her chest, her face even paler than normal. "Oh my God," Kat let out. Mira scanned her for cuts but saw none.

Ray was sprinting toward them, saying something Mira couldn't yet hear, Felissa and Aron just behind him, Aron's camera bouncing by the strap against his hip as he ran.

"You've got some of it in your face." Kat swiveled Mira's head, her fingers on her chin. Nauseous from the adrenaline, Mira mumbled that it stung like crazy and let herself enjoy Kat's concern, pretending for the moment that it negated other things.

Mira looked in the rearview mirror. A shard of glass the size of a thumbtack had lodged at an angle in the center of her cheek.

Ray ran up carrying a first-aid kit, his cellular phone clamped under his armpit. "Are you hurt?" Mira shook her head that she was okay. His eyes shot to Kat.

"I'm fine," she said.

Mira closed her eyes, thinking that would help the nausea. Aron and Felissa walked up to Kat's window.

"Was that from you?" Felissa said toward Ray. A minivan passed by at full interstate speed without moving into the left lane. A burst of hot wind came their way.

"Yeah," Ray said.

"You could've lost control." Mira spotted the dirty stripes on his upper sleeve where he had wiped his face.

Ray shook his head. "I had seventeen tires left." He handed the phone to Aron. "Call the office, would you? Tell 'em we need a windshield installed on-site. They can track down the nearest glass place faster than we can." Most of the windshield was still intact, though fragmented like a mosaic and caved in half a foot or so.

Aron sneaked a picture of Mira's bloody cheek before she could protest. "Merci," he said, cluelessly rolling his *r* Spanish-style. He walked backward as he dialed the number, stopping ten feet away in the rough grass that lined the highway. He stood with arms folded, head tilted toward the sky as he talked.

The first-aid kit was a tackle box filled with individually wrapped medical supplies: Band-Aids, gauze squares, antiseptic pads, cloth tape, aspirin, smelling salts.

"Your secret stash."

"Sure you don't want a doctor?" Ray asked. She leaned up to the rearview mirror. The piece of glass had taken on the look of a ruby, glistening red. Fresh blood dripped down her cheek in two parallel streams.

"It looks pretty shallow," Mira said.

Ray opened a bottle of alcohol the size of an airplane liquor bottle and balanced the cap on her thigh. He held a pair of tweezers out over the ground, then dripped the alcohol over them, the runoff splattering onto his boots. With his hand cupping her chin, he pointed her head at an angle toward him. "I'm just gonna edge it out," he said. Kat cowered into her corner of the pickup, her winces muffled by hands. Felissa leaned in to get a closer look.

Mira closed her eyes and concentrated on the feel of Ray's hand, which she thought was shaking a little. She felt the gentle tug of the tweezers, then the coolness of air entering the small wound left as the glass came out. Ray held the piece up, clasped in the tweezers like a rare gem, or a pulled tooth.

He smiled. "A souvenir?"

"She may have a scar for that," Kat said.

Felissa fingered her own to the right of her lip. "We'll have matching ones."

Ray walked in front of the pickup and unpinched the tweezers, dropping the bloodied chip into the weeds. Aron was walking back, the cell phone in his back pocket. Ray took it out and checked to see if Aron had turned it off.

"What's the word?" Ray asked.

"Closest outfitter is Nashville," Aron said. "Be about two hours before it gets here."

"That's lovely." Kat was sweeping out the glass chips with a whisk broom she had found behind the seat.

"If we complain a lot, they'll get here faster," Aron said her way.

"Rain may beat 'em." Ray arched his neck back and scanned the sky, a dozen shades of gray. It could have been drawn with charcoal. The clouds had thickened and seemed lower, the wind sporadic. Mad gusts faded into wisps, then picked up again. There was no real sunlight left. It was all blue, gray, powdery, cool, and, Mira thought as the five of them hovered just before the downpour, flattering. They looked like romantic ghosts of their real selves, minus the blemishes and imperfections that sunlight insisted on pointing out.

Kat got out of the pickup and sat on the hood next to Aron. Ray wiped the cut with alcohol swabs, which came away pink. The slight sting of the alcohol felt good, the penetrating smell reassuring. Mira could feel Ray's breath against her chin. He seemed to be enjoying the swabbing.

The cut cleaned, he tore open two Band-Aids. Mira held them in the center while he pulled the adhesive off. He positioned them on her cheek, pressing his fingers lightly against her skin to secure them.

Mira felt buzzed, or high on caffeine. "That could've been bad."

"Worse than bad." Ray closed the latches on the tackle box. They walked to the front of the pickup, where Aron was offering Kat his take on tread loss.

"They just keep layerin' new rubber over the existing tires. Be like painting a dresser that's already got several layers on it. Say you don't strip it first, you just go ahead and put a new layer on. It's cheaper and easier and all that, but ten to one, the thing's gonna start peeling a lot sooner than if you'd started fresh with the raw wood."

"So are you pro or con?" If Kat was mocking him, she disguised it well, and Aron didn't detect it.

"It's a tough issue," Aron said. "The retreads are hazards, no question. But imagine having to pay for new tread tires for an eighteen-wheeler; then imagine doin' that five times a year. That'd put a lot of truckers out of business. Especially the independents."

An oil tanker sounded its horn as it gusted by. The driver moved into the left lane, though Ray had pulled the house well off the highway.

"Are we okay here for now?" Mira asked.

"Fine." Then after a pause, Ray said, "Aron, why don't you put some cones behind the truck, just for the hell of it." Aron jogged ahead to get them from the flatbed.

By now, all of the eastbound cars had their headlights on, though most had turned their windshield wipers off. The storm was coming their way. The mass of clouds drifted in tiny increments, almost invisibly, like a giant oil spill in the sky, wreaking havoc on everything in its path.

Ray and Mira sat in the ankle-high weeds just off the shoulder, near the truck. Looking at Kat, he said, "You'll have a winner next show-and-tell, huh, squirrel bait?"

"We have to finish our phonics unit first." Kat poked a finger into her cheek. "No, that's not till the third grade." She followed this with a smile that said she wouldn't hold it against him. "How old are you again?"

"Thirty-two," he said, then added, "and a half."

"Twice as me." Kat's eyes stayed on Ray as he got up to supervise Aron's placement of the hazard cones: three of them at ten-foot intervals behind the pickup, just a few feet off the road. Ray signaled okay with a quick nod of his head.

"What time is it?" Mira asked after a couple of minutes.

"Ten-twenty," Aron said, sitting back on the hood. "Plenty of time." Mira flashed him a confused look.

Felissa had walked back to Aron's truck and stayed gone a few minutes. She came back with a Huckleberry Hound lunch box and took a seat on the hood next to Aron. "Let me do you."

"Excuse?" Aron raised one eyebrow at the lunch box. She unlatched it and started digging into tubes and bottles of cosmetics, then pulled out two shades of foundation and held them up to Aron's cheek, looking for the better match.

"It's time for your summer makeover," she said.

"Shit no." He started picking old crusts of lovebugs off the truck's grille. "Do Kat."

"You know you've always wondered what you'd look like made up." Then, when he wasn't swayed, she leaned into him and, almost too quietly for the rest to hear, said, "Don't be a baby, Baby. Pass me some sugar." She puckered. He rolled his eyes and kissed her, then took off his sunglasses, closed his eyes, and angled his head toward the sky, where a hundred birds spiraled as if caught in a whirlwind, gliding in slow motion, their wings outstretched and still.

Felissa dabbed foundation onto Aron's face with her middle finger. "Let's play a game."

"Let's be hokey," Kat said.

Aron opened his eyes long enough to give Kat a look. "You're a stick in the mud's what you are."

"Somebody come up with a question and everybody has to answer it," Felissa said.

"That's a game?" Ray asked.

"Yeah. Called killing time."

"I'm out." Kat got her sketchbook from the truck, found a tree to lean against, and started drawing.

Mira looked at Felissa. "You start."

"Okay, if you had to lose one of your senses, which would it be and why?"

"Easy," Ray said. "Smell."

"I'm with you," Aron agreed. "Fact, sometimes it'd be a good thing not to be able to smell, around certain people and at certain moments."

"Nope," Mira said. "The smell of smoke is the first sign of fire." She looked over at Kat from twenty feet away. Their eyes met for an instant, and Kat did a weird wiggle with her face, as if to make sure Mira knew that Kat thought they were geeks.

Felissa mouthed *Duh,* then added, "That's what smoke alarms are for."

Ray spotted a dime in the grass and pocketed it. "Battery's been dead in mine for two years."

"There's nothing vital about touch," Mira said. "If you can see, then you don't really need to touch, because anything you couldn't touch, you could see."

"No way," Ray said. "If you can't touch, you can't feel pain. So to know you were hurt, you'd have to have an open wound, or be bleeding or something. Taste is clearly the throwaway."

"How would you know if meat was rancid?" Mira wound a piece of reed grass around her forefinger.

"Expiration dates are good for that," Ray answered. "Plus, it starts to look gelatinous."

"You could smell it anyway," Aron said.

"Can you smell if you can't taste?" Felissa asked.

Ray cocked his head to the side. "Now that you mention it, seems like I usually can't taste as well if I'm congested." They all pondered their experience on this as a convoy of antique Corvettes with Texas tags sped by in the left lane, off to a convention.

Then the rain started. It came suddenly, a wall of it, and everything was cast into a wet shadow. Warm dollops hit them in the face as they all looked up to guess at how long it would last. Ray got up first.

"I'm headin' for the rig."

"We've got shelter there." Aron looked toward Lila. The thick plastic covering its windows sucked in and out with shifts in the wind.

"The trucks'll do fine," Mira said.

But as if they hadn't heard her, the rest were already running behind Aron, headed for the front door, which backed up to the truck's cab. Mira followed, the rain heavier now. Ray fingered the knotted rope that secured the door closed, but he couldn't untie it, so he cut it with the knife on his belt. The door swung open on its own. They walked in and Mira put her shoe in front of the door to keep it closed. The pleasing feel of the hardwood floor—its unfailing coolness, its seams like pinstripes under her bare foot—made her feel ten years old again, like nothing else about Lila had. She slid the other shoe off.

Sketchbook still in hand, Kat was shooting her eyes around, trying to take it all in for the first time.

"You want the tour?" Mira asked.

"I'll opt for the self-guided." Kat started for the kitchen.

The place smelled like the plastic on the windows. The couch, anchored to the floor with rope tied to hooks, was the only furniture in the living room. The seat cushions were indented in the center from years of weight.

"Seems to be traveling well." Ray traced his finger along a stretch of puckering duct tape on a windowsill. The drumming of the rain against the roof sounded like applause.

A minute later, Kat stood with her back to them in the master bedroom, just off the living room, to the right. She was gripping the glass doorknob—it looked like a cut diamond the size of a tennis ball—turning it, then letting it snap back. Her head was aimed at the bed, and Mira realized that she hadn't even straightened the bedspread, which was still creased and puckered diagonally from a few days earlier. Mira's eyes floated up and landed on the marred door frame, scarred from years of Wesley's neck stretching.

Careful not to look Mira's way, Kat walked back into the living room, sat on the hardwood floor a few feet from the couch, and went back to the drawing.

Felissa was sitting cross-legged in front of Aron, close to a window for light. She pulled out a lighter, flicked it, and held it under an eyeliner pencil for an instant.

Aron jerked back and leaned on the balls of his hands. "What the hell?"

"Better coverage," she said.

"Okay, I've got a game." Kat seemed suddenly engaged. "Everybody has to describe their oldest memory."

"You start," Mira said, curious.

"No, I'm going last."

"How can you be sure it's your oldest?" Aron asked.

"Just pretend it is," Ray said.

Mira flinched at a clap of thunder and thought about her habit of taking liberties with early childhood memories, and dreams, for that matter, imposing order that wasn't there, sticking in coherence, when the real thing—or at least her memory of it—was a blur of unrelated nonsense.

Ray spoke up first. "I used to think Miami was a state."

"That's not a memory," Mira told him.

"I remember it."

"It has to be an event," Aron said.

"Then I fold."

"We'll come back to you." Aron's face was just a few inches from Felissa's as she combed his eyebrows with a toothbrush. "I got whipped when I was four for swinging a kid too high on the swing set. I got him so he was almost parallel to the ground on the up-swing and crying to get down, and course after awhile, the other kids formed a circle around me, just watching, which is what any kid wants, so I kept it up till Miss Linda came out with the Ping-Pong paddle and yanked me away by the elbow." He paused for Felissa to apply the lipstick, then went on. "My dad locked me in the garage for the next two days, only let me in to sleep and use the toity. The worst was that he used to make sauerkraut in a big Crock-Pot, ferment the cabbage right there in the garage. Damned if it didn't smell worse than it tasted."

Ray was switching a small flashlight on his key chain on and off. "That explains your sauerkraut issue."

"You deserved every whiff," Felissa almost whispered.

Mira went along. "Remind me never to approach a merry-go-round you're on."

"I was four," Aron said defensively. Felissa finished his mascara, then pulled out a safety pin and started toward his lashes. Aron let out a mock yell.

Felissa turned his head toward the gray light let in by the windows. "Trust me."

Ray slapped his thighs like he had just gotten an idea. "When I was still in diapers, I found my dad trapped in a rocking chair by my mother. She had the thing pulled back, just resting on the points of the legs, and she was bent down, yelling in his face, I was too young to understand what about. He kept trying to squirm up, but he's a pretty heavy guy. Then she let go and he got the wind knocked out of him."

"I don't imagine Wayne would want that to get around," Mira said.

Ray shook his head. "Actually, he'd be the first to tell you the story."

"My go," Felissa said. "When I was a little kid, we spent summers in our RV in Florida selling fireworks for the Fourth of July, and no matter how many times Dad bombed the place, it was still a jumbo roach convention, like ones the size of human ears. And one night the lights were out and everyone was asleep but me and I see this mondo cockroach crawling across the orange lit face of the alarm clock, on the inside, like it had gotten in through a crack."

"Roaches get a bad rap," Aron said. "I once got a free meal at Pizza Hut because a roach fell from the ceiling onto our bread sticks."

"You should start taking one along when you go out to eat," Ray suggested. "Let him loose just as the waitress comes with the check."

"BYOR." Felissa laughed with a straight face.

Ray nudged his foot into Mira's calf. "Your turn."

"Mine's almost as graphic."

"Graphic's good," Ray told her.

"Okay. Throwing up a beet," Mira said. "I was exploring between the fridge and the wall—I'm not sure for what—and I found this beet sliver, kind of slimy and darker than your normal beet, but that didn't rule it out for me, so I was in midchew when my mother found me and started probing her finger around to get out what she could, but I'd already swallowed most of it. Then a few minutes later, I got sick on their bedroom carpet."

"That carpet?" Ray pointed to the master bedroom.

"That's the one." Aron leaned into the floor and made a mock vomiting noise. "Mom came in and cleaned it up, yelled at me some more, then sent me to bed with no dinner. But Dad sneaked me some powdered Gatorade and saltines before he went to bed, said it would settle my stomach. It was the sweetest."

"This is a real shame." Ray faked some mixture of disgust and disappointment. "I'd always been a beet person."

Felissa waved a flattened hand under Aron's face. "Comments?"

"You've got a certain Loretta Swit quality," Mira said.

"Do you feel aroused?" Ray asked Aron.

But before Aron could answer, Kat started in, her stare at Mira so intent, the two of them might as well have been alone in the room. "Okay, I'm six and I'm sorting through this Buster Brown shoe box full of reject photos—you know, like the ones that never made it into the albums. And I find this one picture of an old house, kind of freaky-looking. So I go to Mom and ask her whose house it is, and she just stands there thinking for a sec, like she can't quite make the connection. Then it dawns on her that it belonged to her sister, Kat for short, the one I was named after. So she tells me about how Kat died when she was twenty-five—that part, I already knew—and says the house was sold after Aunt Kat's death and then torn down so the land could be farmed. Then Mom says she knew when she got pregnant with me that I was her sister's angel coming back to her, and that that made her love me in a particular way that she couldn't manage with anyone else. So I say, 'Can I go by Kat from now on?' And by this time, Mom can barely talk, 'cause we're both crying by now, but she manages to get out, 'Nothing would make me happier.'"

Something in Kat's stare made it clear to Mira that the game had been calculated, not an accident, but a measured retaliation. No one said anything. From outside, the weather was speaking to their senses: the shadowy blue, barely there light, the bitter smell of over-sized raindrops, the feel of the hardwood floor as it vibrated to the stuttering thunder, all this to the even crackle of the rain, like static from a Victrola. In this case, Ray had been right. Taste was nowhere in the picture, save the phantom flavor of beets, tangy and rotten, against Mira's four-year-old tongue.

 *Thirteen*

They had pulled the windshield repairman away from a round of golf. His white glove poked halfway out of his back pocket. He looked like Dom DeLuise, except that his right hand was absent a pinkie. When he sensed that Aron took particular notice of this, he said, "Thank God for workman's comp." He paused and crunched at the gravel with his metal cleats, as if considering asking about the makeup—which Aron apparently had forgotten about—then thought better of it and wished them a fine day.

The clouds had broken into stringy fragments, marbleizing the blue sky that had begun to appear. Water had collected in the road's parallel indentations—more pronounced in the right lane—there from years of traffic. The rain had washed the film off of everything, leaving the trees a deep waxy green, the road like a stream of black coal, still steaming from the rain. The grime of days of driving had been sheared from the trucks: Beige became white, brown became gold, and dull gray became chrome. Everything shined.

Back on the road, as if she had done her verbal damage for the day, Kat continued to make some point—Mira wasn't quite sure yet what it was—with silence and an even stare out the window. For a while, Mira played with the idea that Kat felt guilty, like she had overdone it. Then Kat's flash of a grin to herself convinced Mira that she was replaying her monologue instead, savoring the stunned looked on Mira's face, just the one she had been aiming for.

After a while, Kat went back to the sketchbook and Mira caught a look at what she was working on, a courtroom scene in serious colors, browns and beiges and golds. A prosecutor with a receding chin and hairline to match leaned into the stand, his face a foot away from the witness, her brown hair in a secretarial bun, a tissue in each hand. The judge, half-reclined in a chair twice her size, rested her head on a single index finger as she listened. The jurors were faceless torsos.

Knowing she might be ignored, Mira asked anyway, "Which one am I?"

"Good courtroom artists don't use symbolism." Kat added handlebars to the bailiff's mustache. "You're the stenographer."

A couple of hours from the Arkansas border, they stopped at a rest area for a construction update. Ray had heard word over the CB of some median work they might run into. Felissa ambled into the pet rest area and tried to engage a pug in baby talk. Kat stayed in the pickup.

Inside, the rest stop had the couchy feel of a furniture showroom, or a model home. Heirloom portraits of the governor and attorney general hung over a gas fireplace, wishing safe travel. Mira and Ray were greeted with some version of hello by three oldish women behind the counter, each in microphone headsets. One was in charge of beverages and offered them a soda or coffee. Another asked Ray to sign the guest list. The third woman was bent over a

map laid out on the counter. An elderly man watched as she highlighted a route in fluorescent yellow, tracing it with the pinkie of
her other hand.

Mira walked to the tiered shelves of travel brochures, immacu-
lately organized into regions, then grouped alphabetically into Dining, Lodging, Outdoor, and Shopping. A slouchy teenager added
one of each to the stack of dozens already in his hand. Mira remembered a similar stash she and Kearney had stored in the pocket
behind the Fury's front seat. They had grown to revere them like
baseball cards: negotiating trades, estimating worth, valuing some
more than others. Despite the waste, their parents had supported
the habit, Wesley arguing that collecting was healthy for kids, Helen
saying she would encourage a free source of easy car amusement
any day compliments of the State Tourism Board.

"We're in the clear." Ray had stepped up behind Mira and spoke
over her shoulder as she scanned the shelves. "Only one lane in the
eastbound."

Mira was in the Lodging section: The Sure-Rest Inn, Pearl's
Overnight, View O' the Mountain Lodge. She picked up a brochure
for Bernice's B and B in Gatlinburg, a pseudo-Victorian crowded
between two others.

"You been there?" Ray asked.

"The town?" Mira said. He nodded. "Nope. My parents went
once and Mom would never go back, said the quaint quotient was
too high."

Ray conveyed with a slow blink of his eyes and nod of his head
that he could relate to this.

"Be nice to be on our own for a while," Mira said.

"That it would."

Mira was trying to see how long she could hold Ray's stare, when

Aron walked up. He had just washed the makeup off, and Mira used her thumb to wipe a patch of soap from his sideburn.

She slipped the underwater pictures from Aron's shirt pocket. They had stopped for gas at the Wal-Mart exit to pick them up.

"I got *dobles*," Aron said.

The picture of the four of them had been slid into the oval display window of the blue plastic envelope. They were in shadow, the round light glowing from behind. Tiny bubbles perked out from between Ray's smiling lips. Mira clung to him with a hand hooked over the arm he had straightened to anchor her. Her cheeks were inflated, her neck hidden behind her shirt, which was ballooned out like a spinnaker. Aron held Kat down with a hand on her head. Her face was lost behind the rush of bubbles shooting out of her mouth, her knees floating up toward her chin. She looked as if she was drowning.

Aron held the photo out at arm's length. "I call it *Human Aquarium Decor.*"

Back in the pickup, as Kat feigned sleep, Mira let herself imagine a trip to Gatlinburg with Ray, how such a trip might go. She would tell him how she always felt untouchable in a rental car, all insured and cushioned and automatically locked in, sealed off from wind and engine noise, shaded with just the right amount of tint—the closest she had ever come to being in a sensory-deprivation chamber. So he would surprise her and rent a car, opting for the upgrade, a Pontiac Grand Am or a Ford Taurus.

They would leave at sunrise with a full thermos and two beaker-shaped travel mugs with nonslip bottoms. They would take turns driving, and whoever wasn't behind the wheel would pour and navigate. They would stay on two-lane roads for variety's sake, which would put them into Gatlinburg later, but they would decide that was okay.

Once there, they would spend two days evaluating the mini-golf scene, rationing their intake of saltwater taffy, weighing barbecue versus catfish. At first, they would be charmed by the bluegrass, then notice that it was everywhere, that they couldn't get away from it, as if it were piped in townwide, and this would become funny after a while, their first private joke. As they meandered their way down streets named for country-music pioneers, Ray would stop her after so long and kiss her, and they would do this every few blocks. Then they would rejoin the flow of the crowd into fancy craft stores and overpriced souvenir shops, which soon enough would all look the same, but they would end up buying gourmet corn-bread mix and a make-your-own-dulcimer kit anyway.

After awhile, Mira would start to find something sensual in everything about Ray. The way he whistled without even knowing he was doing it. The way his face got flushed after his first glass of red wine. The swirls of hair at the base of his neck. The curve of his hand as it came to rest on the steering wheel, or a glass. The way he used his arm as a headrest, slung back and bent behind his head, and made this look as natural as crossed legs.

Their last night there, she would wake up in their skinny motel bed, to find Ray wide-awake and staring at her. They would have motel sex; then she would focus on looking pretty as she drifted back off to sleep. Then, on the next day's drive home, she would replay everything, and from the tiny spontaneous smiles Ray would break into when he thought she wasn't looking, Mira would know that he was doing the same thing.

———

That night, Mira called Kearney to let him know they would be home the next day. After she filled him in on the logistics, he asked how she was doing.

"I'm pretty okay."

"Pretty?" Kearney repeated. She was propped up on two pillows, lying on her back, staring at the stains like coffee spills on the low ceiling.

"I feel like I've been double-parked for the past six months."

"They're gonna have a warrant out for your arrest."

"You're my bail connection," Mira said. "How's business?"

"I had to bail out the counterfeiter again today. He was so grateful, palmed me a hundred-dollar bill and told me to send my enemies to the bank with it."

Mira figured she knew what Kearney was looking for next when he asked how other things were going, but Kat was there, watching *Rescue 911*, so Mira's answers stayed general.

Then he said, "I know about the dead man." When Mira didn't say anything, he went on. "You got a message this morning from the investigator guy. I hope you don't mind me returning the call."

"Sorry," Mira told him. "I figured I'd just tell you when we got home."

"Turns out the guy was a flight case from a minimum-security gig. His family told him to get lost, so he crossed the northern border."

"From Canada?"

"Virginia."

"What did he die of?" Mira glanced at Kat, who was busy fol-

lowing a dramatization of a preschooler finding his mother unconscious in the bathtub.

"They ruled it cardiac arrest, but he'd been living off pears for
several weeks. Is that tree still there?"

"What was his name?" Mira asked.

"Paul something. Bernard, I think." She could hear the rattle of
ice as Kearney took a drink of something. "So how's Lila?"

"Same as ever," she answered.

Off the phone, Mira braced for questions from Kat, but none
came. On TV, the kid actor was following a dispatcher's instructions
to drain the tub and find blankets, voice-overs filling the gaps in
the 911 tape.

Mira pretended to watch, aiming her eyes on the paneled wall
just above the TV. She thought of Paul Bernard loitering in the
living room, then the kitchen, waiting for something to hit him
differently, something new to think about. As he stepped across the
hardwood floors, he would pay special attention to the rattle of the
light fixtures, or bulbs loose in their sockets. He would compare
the echo of his voice in one room to another, feel silly at first, then
realize there's no need for that when you're as alone as a body can
be. Every time he walked down the hallway, he would slap the pull
cord that hung from the disappearing stairway to the attic, and he
would grow to take comfort in this tiny ritual. With no electricity,
he would go to bed at dusk and, in the receding light, study the
textured ceiling, look for faces in it, find a profile, or a foot, or the
shape of Africa. He would listen to what had always been described
to him as the sound of a house settling: wood warping, roof tiles
clicking as they cooled off. Then, with nothing to look forward to
but sleep, he would do exactly as she had at seventeen and pregnant.

He would lie there wishing it on himself in what were the best moments of the day.

Mira waited until she thought Kat was asleep, then got out of bed, turned on the air conditioner to dull the noise, got dressed, and left the motel room. It was midnight.

Ray's room was a few doors down. She knocked, and after a minute or so, it was Aron who cracked the chained door, still hazy from sleep. When he saw it was Mira, he unchained it. Mira walked in. Felissa was fully dressed and splayed stomach-down on the bed closest to the window. On the other bed, Ray was on his side, his left arm pointed straight in front of him.

"Ray." Mira nudged his shoulder, which twitched, but he didn't wake up. She shook his elbow. This time, he shifted, then turned over and looked at her through squinting eyes. The only light came from the parking lot, so he could barely make her out.

"What's the matter?" His voice came out in knots.

"Come with me."

He lay still for a few more seconds, let out a quick groan that she tried not to take personally, then nudged the covers off with his feet. He slid his jeans over his boxer shorts, and Mira pulled him by the hand out of the room. Aron had gone back to the bed and was leaning against the headboard, burying his hand in Felissa's hair as he watched them leave.

The parking lot, close to empty a few hours earlier, had filled up with late-night arrivals. In the buzzy light, Mira could make out the imprint of sheet creases on the side of Ray's face.

"Are you sleepwalking?" Ray asked.

"Wide-awake," Mira said over her shoulder.

They walked to the back, where the house was parked. Ray lifted himself onto the flatbed in the space between the house and the cab, then reached down and pulled her up behind him. Inside, Mira led the way to the back bedroom, the one with the sloped ceiling. The house was almost solid black, but she knew the way, as if all the lights were on. In her room, the twin bed she had slept on as a child was exactly where it had always been, directly below the room's only window, which let in a dim, cloudy light. The mattress was bare, the original fabric—orange and brown flowers against a white background—yellowed by time and sporadic bed-wetting.

The only other furniture in the room was a dressing table Mira had had as long as she could remember. Designed for a child, it sat low to the floor, with two drawers on each side and a round mirror the size of a tire in the middle. The stool, now secured to the dresser with bungee cords, was only a foot and a half high. Its metal legs, made to mimic the legs of a ballet dancer in midplié, had always hit Mira as sad, as if the dresser had been meant for some ten-year-old prima ballerina, someone other than her.

She lay down on the mattress, and Ray followed her, lying on his side, his arm bent to prop up his head. He seemed wide-awake now, and after a minute, he said, "I bet you were a sweet thing sleeping in this bed." His lips were still moving with the words when he leaned his head down and gave her a small kiss, like a theater kiss, where little contact is made, just enough to convey to the audience the general idea.

"I'm gonna worry about you," he told her.

"I'm just helping you decide."

"How's this faring?" He skimmed his lips around the bandage on her cheek.

"It needs attention," she said, and they let themselves go into a tangle of one thing against another. That close to Ray, webbed with him like held hands, Mira felt like a near beginner, not fumbling or at a loss, but stunned by his pressure, the novelty of him, and the startling intimacy of eyes open, making contact, taking all this in. The feel of him amazed her, though he felt exactly as she had imagined he would.

Afterward, they looked for art in the shards and geometrics of light that made their way in through the window. Outside, diesel engines crescendoed as they approached on the interstate, their drone growing louder and clarifying, then fading just as quickly as they drove out of earshot. It was either this sound or the half-conscious state they were both in, as if they had been anesthetized and the effect hadn't quite worn off, that kept them from hearing someone come into the house. That they weren't alone only became clear when Kat's faint outline appeared in the doorway to the bedroom, clad in her jeans and Mira's shirt, shoeless.

"Can this be my room?" Kat asked. Ray reached for his jeans on the floor. Mira tucked her arms and legs in, shriveling into a ball, as if this would do any good. Kat was already feeling her way back down the hall.

"Come back," Mira half-yelled, though she knew that wasn't what needed to happen. Knowing better, Kat kept going.

Before she made the turn out of sight, Kat yelled, "Slobs," and it echoed through the shell of a house. Mira watched Kat's ghostlike blur in shades of gray as it faded into the blackness of the living room.

Still before sunrise, as Ray slept and Mira lay awake, both in the bed where Kat had found them, having decided that a return to the motel room would make things worse, Mira did what she always did when she wanted something to happen that she knew never would. She imagined every bit of it as she waited for sleep to hit her, played it out in woozy detail, this time in dramatization form, and hoped it would make a cameo in a dream later on.

She pictured an actress who bore the requisite resemblance to her, then a house that could pass for Lila. She imagined the actress lifting a five-gallon gas can, realizing it was too heavy to carry around, so funneling some of the gasoline into a frog-shaped watering can. Fume swirls would loft toward her as she poured.

She would start with the living room and trail the gasoline along the exposed baseboards, like pesticide, and finish this off with random splashes in the center of the room. She would go to the kitchen and do the same. Then, in what was supposed to be Mira's bedroom, Mira's look-alike would pause significantly and gaze at her make-believe ten-year-old self, HOLLY HOBBY splayed across the back of her exposed panties, limbs bent as she slept, mouth agape, only the whites of her eyes showing through barely cracked eyelids. The camera would zoom in as the gasoline flowed out in a nice arc. Mira imagined this part twice, the second time focusing on the quiet slap of the gasoline hitting the hardwood floor.

A car alarm in the motel parking lot brought Mira out of a half sleep, and she recalled a comic strip magnetted to Kearney's refrigerator as long as he had been old enough to own one. A bloated, goofy yardman carries a gas can with a hole in it, unknowingly fueling an entire yard, which in the next frame is ablaze. The yardman miraculously survives. His clothes cling to him by charred threads. His skin is the color of charcoal, a sharp contrast to his eyes, which are bright white, wide, and dumb to what happened and why.

Mira went back to the scene, where the actress would be lighting the first match next to the open front door. Mira liked the idea of the breeze blowing it out, so she imagined that, then imagined enjoying the leftover smell. The woman would strike another and let go. The fire would ignite before the match hit the floor, as if the gasoline had risen up to meet it.

She would make a mad grab for her purse—a prop—then close the front door behind her and start toward the road. Within a few seconds, she would hear puffs of new flame, like sheets being fluffed out from the dryer. As the fire grew, so did her alarm at her own actions, the voice-over would say. She would pick up the pace as she got to the road and turn left toward the highway. Only then would she look back at the house. Thick blackness would've filled the picture window like an ash curtain, too perfect for a dream or real life. Smoke would pump out of the ducts and eaves. She would walk faster.

After a quarter of a mile, the road would curve. About to lose sight of the house, she would look at it for the last time, orange flames quivering an impossible hundred feet into the sky, shooting up in shivers, ebbing and flowing, like waves of sleep, unsure of whether to thrive or subside, wavering back and forth between the two.

Fourteen

At seven the next morning, after Mira had drummed up the nerve to go back to the room so that she and Kat could carefully sidestep one another, the group convened in the motel lobby. Mira lagged behind to pick up a newspaper, wanting Ray and Kat to have their privacy as they got whatever they were going to say or not say out of their systems. Then, over their last continental breakfast, Aron started in on the fake wake-up calls he had made that morning. Mira scanned the room to see if any of his victims were within earshot. Other than a teenage kid wearing a supercollider T-shirt, who seemed to be eyeing Kat, no one was paying any attention.

"Rise and Shine, sleepyheads." Aron fashioned a phone with his pinkie and thumb. "Time to get up. If you don't get out of bed, either you're gonna do some butt kissin' or I'm gonna do some butt kickin'." He squeezed his eyes shut and let out a whistley laugh, the kind you would expect from an old drinker.

Ray reached over and slid Aron's coffee cup away from him. "That'll be enough for now." Unfazed, Aron wiped his eyes from the laugh, took his cup back, and got up for a refill.

Before they got back on the road, Aron checked the oil in the trucks and tugged at the chains at the base of Lila, Kat got a root beer from next door, and Ray kissed Mira—for moral support, he said—as they were shielded behind the house. His ETA had them in Mims by 1:00 P.M.

Mira was strapped in before she spotted Kat heading for Aron's truck. He noticed, said something to Kat, she said something back, and he looked toward Mira to get her take on this. Felissa slid to the middle to make room for Kat. Ray waved them ahead.

At the motel exit, Mira pulled up behind Ray, then got out of her pickup and walked to Aron's. Kat saw Mira coming and reached to lock the doors with balled fists. But Aron's window was cracked enough for Mira to reach in and unlock the door, and when she did, he and Felissa got out and squatted in the grassy island at the front of the motel. Mira sat down behind the wheel, half-expecting Kat to get out, but she stayed put.

"Last night was dumb," Mira said.

"I'm sure Ray would be flattered." Kat was studying a lock of her hair, yanking out the ones with split ends.

"Of me, your queenliness. It was dumb of me."

A quick honk came from behind. Mira glanced in the rearview mirror and saw that they were blocking several cars. She planted one foot on the pavement. "I dropped the ball, okay?" Kat ignored her, making a big deal about where her backpack was situated at her feet. "Don't make this bigger than it has to be," Mira said, knowing this remark wouldn't suffice.

"And how big does it have to be?"

Mira struck a puzzled look. "I don't know how to answer that question." A slimy man in a BMW pulled around them, coming within a hair of Mira's open door just to make a point.

"Neither do I." Kat reached over and honked the horn in three quick bursts, a signal to Aron and Felissa that the conversation was over.

They had a couple of hours of interstate left; then they would cut south and be on two-lanes the rest of the way to Mims. Soon after they crossed the Mississippi, the scenery took on the look of Arkansas. The few houses built within sight of the highway had storm cellars off to the side. The first John Deere dealership they came to was fronted by a yard display of antique tractors next to late models, glossy green and yellow. The land flattened into delta. Signs of farming were everywhere.

A white government-owned sedan approached at twice Mira's speed, then slowed. The poufy-haired man on the passenger side seemed to want a closer look. Through a wide smile, he talked into a cell phone and looked with slits for eyes at Lila, then Mira, then back at Lila. She wondered what he was saying, whether he would go home and tell his wife and kids over fish sticks about the house he had seen on the interstate, an odd one at that. She figured that he would, that he would immortalize them in that way, like strangers caught in someone else's vacation photo. He clapped his phone shut with his chin, then flicked the nub of a lit cigarette out the window. Mira could still remember the exact feeling she would get as a child when she would catch someone at this, her trembly sense of certain disaster as she watched the cigarette flitter away like a lightning bug. She recalled counting the seconds until the thing bobbed right into the door of the gas tank, made the slightest contact with a dried strand of gasoline, how she thought that's all it would take for them all to ignite in a flash. She had never actually seen this happen, but it had seemed to her only a matter of time, chances being what she figured they were.

A layer of haze had locked the heat in. Mira rolled down her window partway. Her skin had already taken on the stickiness that would linger all day. Her hair was unruly from the humidity and wind of the day before. Beyond the densest layer, which was pulled tight into a ponytail, was an inch-thick atmosphere of frizz. She explored this with her fingers as she drove.

They rounded a soft turn in the interstate. About a quarter mile ahead was a row of brake lights. Mira reached for the CB.

"You see that stoppage ahead?" She knew Ray saw it because the flatbed's brake lights had come on. When he didn't respond, she tried again, this time using both of their handles. Still nothing.

The string of cars stretched over a slight hill that blocked her from seeing what the holdup was. Toward the front, drivers had given up on a quick go-ahead and turned off their engines. As she slowed, she pictured the aftermath of a crash she had seen as a kid on a two-lane road just outside of Mims. A Pinto station wagon had hit a telephone pole head-on and curved around the pole like a horseshoe around a stake, its front half cut in two. A heavy spray of blood had given the shattered front windshield the look of stained glass. As they drove by, crawling as if in a funeral procession, her father had admonished her and Kearney not to look, but at the last second, she had anyway. The thing was so mangled, it seemed as unreal as a cartoon.

It wasn't until Mira stopped just behind Ray that he came back over the CB. The drivers in front of them had already turned off their engines and were milling around, exchanging theories on the cause of the delay, she figured.

"Sorry about that," Ray said. "I was on the cell." And Mira knew when he didn't volunteer it that he had been talking to Liz.

"So is she coming?" Mira asked. Aron had gotten out of his pickup and was talking to the driver of a Sunbeam bread truck.

"Took some persuading."

"She didn't want to?"

"She asked me why in the world I wanted her to meet me for a house delivery, and I just stuttered something about supper afterward, but she kept pressing me on what the deal was."

"What'd you tell her?"

"That I missed her."

"What'd she say to that?"

"Nothing." Mira thought she could hear Ray scratching his stubble. "She started crying."

"So she'll be there?"

"Plans to be."

Off the CB, Mira put her shoes back on in slow motion. She imagined Liz crying and figured she was one of those people who looks beautiful when they cry. Her face would flush in just the right way. The tears would make her lashes shiny and doll-like, her eyes glassy and sweet. She imagined Ray comforting Liz, knew he would be good at that. Then it occurred to her that Ray had never seen her cry, and now probably never would. Liz was coming around.

Mira joined the rest at the front of Ray's truck. "Any word?"

"Evidently some sort of standoff." Ray held her stare for an extra second, as if he were trying to read her.

Kat looked spooked. "Like what?"

" 'Sall I know," Ray told her. "Maybe I'll skip ahead a little and see what the deal is."

"We'll come along." Aron lifted his cap long enough to smooth back his hair pointlessly. "There's no action here."

"Kat and I'll watch and ward."

The three of them headed out, stopping a few cars up to talk to another truck driver, this one with a parrot balanced on his shoulder. A late-model Ford Mustang a few car lengths ahead drove across the median and turned back east.

Kat was trying to remove a splinter from her palm, maybe leftover glass from the windshield. "Need some help?" Mira asked.

Kat didn't look up. "I'm just browsing."

Mira started for the pickup, passing Lila's right side. The rectangles—ten feet in the air, in full sunlight, overexposed—somehow hit Mira in a different way, like an Easter Seals greeting card, its awkwardness taking on an accidental elegance once you learn it was designed by a schoolkid. And thinking about it now, she figured that that was one of the luxuries of being a child: Your spastic art and clumsiness and all-around bad judgment are forgiven, even praised, just because you're a kid. Instead of getting credit for life experience, you get a handshake for the lack of it.

Mira turned around and walked to the cab of Ray's truck. Kat lay flat on the hood, arms crossed over her face. Mira pulled herself into the cab with the bar there for the purpose. Inside, in a drawer under Ray's seat, underneath road maps, pepper spray, an economy pack of sugarless gum, and a deck of Pennzoil cards, she found a thick roll of reflective orange tape about three inches wide.

Mira went back out, got into the pickup, and edged it between the flatbed and the row of cars in the left lane, with several feet to spare; the drivers had pulled toward the median for a clearer view ahead. She stopped the pickup just to the right of Kearney's rectangle, then stepped into the bed and onto the roof of the cab.

She clawed to find the end of the tape, which was perforated every two feet. She tore off the first strip and pasted it even with the top of the other two rectangles. She kept this up until the tape formed a third. From a few feet away, the thing looked electric in the midmorning sun, a mixed glow of orange and yellow and gold.

Mira waited there until she heard the clap of flip-flops, then turned around and found Kat standing there, arms folded across her chest, T-shirt tied into a knot just above her belly button.

Mira twitched her head toward the rectangle. "All yours."

Kat gave Mira a smile that said she knew what Mira was up to, that she refused to be charmed. Then, with crafted sarcasm, she said, "Consider me moved."

"You looked bored," Mira said, suddenly feeling foolish, but Kat was already walking away, hands busy redoing her ponytail.

A woman in the left lane had her artificially tanned leg extended out the open passenger window of her Acura, her toenails painted the color of bubble gum. Her fingers, a ring on every one, their long nails painted the same way, kneaded the skin on her right kneecap. She was looking Mira's way, and Mira knew that she had witnessed the whole pathetic thing from behind her mirrored sunglasses.

At that moment, Mira felt as if she bore the burden for the world's hokiness, for every long-distance dedication and lifetime achievement award and tribute album and honorary doctorate and reunion tour. She was the poster child for childishness, the spokesperson for the cause.

The toenail woman was still watching. In her glasses, Mira spotted her own reflection: elongated, distorted, and framed by the glowing rectangle.

Mira sat on the hood of the pickup and tried to be distracted by an excessively cute preschooler a few car lengths ahead. He was showing off his Frankenstein's monster walk, aluminum cans molded to the soles of his tennis shoes.

A few minutes later, Mira spotted Ray heading back their way, his face blank, eyes aimed at the intermittent yellow lines at his feet. Felissa and Aron trailed behind him. Swirls of heat lofted off the car roofs on either side. Mira sat up on the hood of the pickup.

"Is it bad?" she asked as Ray got within a few feet.

"It's not a wreck. Be better off if it were." He stood there in front of Mira in his particular way: hand on hip, fingers draped down from belt, all weight on one leg, other leg resting forward. He looked lovelier than she wanted him to.

"It's a hostage situation," he went on. Kat walked up behind him to get the update. "The guy's handcuffed himself to a woman. They've each got a foot in a bucket; cop said it's full of water. He's got a harpoon gun."

"The cop?" Mira asked.

"No, the man."

"Define," Kat said.

"Like an arrow you shoot, but it's attached by a cord to the gun itself. He's got the metal head aimed at a power-line tower. He's threatening to fry himself and the girl."

"What's he want?" Mira asked.

"That, I don't know. Cops won't let anyone within a hundred feet. We might be here till the thing's over."

"Crapola." Felissa lifted her mane of hair and fanned the back of her neck. "What's gonna happen when five hundred cars full of morning coffee drinkers get stranded with no bathroom?"

"The fertilizer crew'll get a week off." Aron thumped a drumroll on the hood.

A few minutes later, word spread that a refrigerated dairy truck a quarter mile back had lost its generator, so the driver was giving away his cargo. Felissa said she was lactose-intolerant. The rest decided to go have a look, except Kat, who turned back at the last minute. "Just bring me back an orange push-up."

Kat was on the bumper, drawing stick-figure cowboys, when Felissa sat down next to her and did a Cher-like swing of her hair. "Do my caricature."

After a few seconds, Kat turned sideways, with just one leg on the road to prop her up, then started drawing.

"What kind of word is *caricature,* anyway?" Felissa arced her neck. "Caricature. Caricature. Caricature. Sounds goofy when you say it over and over."

Kat readjusted the angle of Felissa's head. "All words are like that."

"You should be one of those sketch artists and draw fugitives."

"Forensic art sucks," Kat said. "It's mostly computerized now. They've got these databases with every possible hairline, every eyebrow, every everything. From one database, they can spit out five billion composites. No drawing necessary."

Kat sketched a faint outline of Felissa's face, then filled it in with soft, wide swipes of transparent beige.

She went on: "Now even the computer jobbies are becoming obsolete because they've come out with these sets of transparency cards, and each one shows a different feature, every possible feature you can imagine. These cops carry them around in the trunk, so when they get to a crime scene, the witness describes the suspect, the cop pulls out a card with a low hairline or a receding chin or whatever, sticks it on a portable light table, and waits for the witness to yell bingo. They've got a wanted bulletin in minutes."

"Oh my God." Felissa had a death grip on Kat's wrist as she looked down at the picture. "Oh my God, oh my God. By Jesus, I've got it. I'll send this to my parents with a ransom note."

Kat let out a clipped laugh and matched Felissa's eyes to one of the greens. "Right. I'm a kidnapper, and I'm gonna target the daughter of an RV-living fireworks salesman."

"Please don't underestimate my worth. You're in the company of the sole heiress to the Scodie pyrotechnic fortune."

"Fine, so if I were a kidnapper, why wouldn't I just take a Polaroid?"

Felissa hugged her own head and squealed. "That's the genius of my plan! You're greedy *and* psychotic. You're a crazed artist, which'll freak my parents out way, way more than if you were a just typical bottom-line professional. You sit around in various states of undress and drink cognac and mull over how to render me next. You're a musing kidnapper. The worst-possible kind."

Kat stopped drawing, did a baton twirl with her pencil, then looked at Felissa. "So are you completely, somewhat, slightly, or not at all serious?"

Felissa guided Kat's hand back to the drawing. "The first one. Now be sure you get this in there." Felissa fingered the scar below her lip. "Bottle rocket. My dad's the one who lit it. His guilt got me my first car. Got a lot of mileage out of both."

"That's lovely of you." Kat imagined a grid of a dozen noses, looked at Felissa's—a little too round and turned up at the end—then drew one more like her own, straight and thin, like a beak.

"Guilt's a bargaining tool, see. I figure running away, blaming it on my dad's affair, that'll net me a new CD player. Not like getting scarred for life, but it's worth something."

"What happens when they figure you out?" Kat darkened the green eyes to chocolate.

"I'll fake a nervous breakdown and get a satellite dish." Kat gave Felissa a look like she had just cut off an ambulance. Felissa got the message. "It's not like I've left them for good. Only until June thirtieth."

"What's June thirtieth?" Kat touched a finger to her tongue and softened Felissa's scar until it was nothing more then a shadow.

"Quarterly inventory," Felissa answered. "They'll never stop needing me."

Back from the walk, which netted them a dozen ice-cream sandwiches, Mira asked if anyone wanted to have a closer look at the standoff. Kat surprised her when, after a pause, she stepped down from the hood and mumbled something about needing to move around.

They didn't talk as they walked to the police line, not quite a mile away. At least half of the vehicles sat empty, their owners wandering nearby. A young couple lay on their sides facing each other on a royal blue tarp in the median. The jingle of keys and change in pockets came from a semicircle of slacks-clad men just off the shoulder. A cluster of teenagers—all dressed in the remnants of a marching band's uniforms—had climbed on top of a school bus for a better view of the action ahead. A man and woman sat on top of an oil tanker, straddling the cylinder-shaped tank as they scanned the scene twenty feet below and around them.

The traffic had also been stopped on the eastbound side. A few people had crossed over and were staking out the scene from lawn chairs in the vacant lanes.

Kat and Mira found an opening along the police line. The harpoon man and his hostage, both in their twenties, Mira guessed, stood a hundred feet away, just off the right shoulder, linked by handcuffs. The woman's free hand seemed to be propping her head up. The man held the harpoon by the shaft and stood erect and ready to act, feet a shoulder length apart. He swiveled his head, scanning for any sudden movement. They were just below one in a row of power-line towers that looked like sci-fi movie props without the papier mâché.

About fifty feet away, a perimeter of uniformed officers—Highway Patrolmen, sheriffs, city police, ATF officials—stood or perched one knee to the ground, hands poised on the guns in their holsters. The cops were so still, the scene could've been a photo, or a monument to slain law-enforcement agents.

Then the guy with the harpoon reached into his back pocket and pulled out a portable CB radio. It took a minute for Mira to spot whom he was talking to, a man in a suit sitting in the front seat of a patrol car parked next to an idling ambulance. He chewed madly on a piece of gum as he negotiated.

"FBI," a man next to Kat said, apparently for the benefit of the video camera he cradled on his shoulder.

The two men spoke into the radios, too far away for Mira and Kat to decipher what they said. The woman was doubled over now and they could just barely hear her wailing. The harpoon man jerked his right arm, the one that was handcuffed to her, so that the cuffs must've dug into her wrist. She bolted upright and froze.

An athletic, big-haired woman wearing an ATF windbreaker,

despite the heat, approached the line of observers, swept her arms toward the area behind them, and said, "Folks, orders are to back this line up." When no one moved right away, she ducked under the yellow tape and started tapping people on the shoulder. Other officers had already begun to put up a new line fifty feet back, which would take everyone from within eyesight of the scene. Dejected, the crowd meandered back toward their cars. A woman in a Pizza Hut uniform said to no one in particular, "That hacks me off."

Kat steered Mira into the median, which smelled of being freshly mowed. Discarded grass clippings, too new to have turned brown, formed tractor-width rows. Mira walked right next to Kat, close enough for their shoulders to brush, and Kat didn't walk ahead or move away. Mira took this as a sign that she was open to mulling things over.

And she knew she was right when Kat said, "Way to endear me to the house." She was kicking a half-empty plastic bottle of Sprite ahead of her as she went.

"This has nothing to do with Lila. Nothing does really." Mira said this as if it were obvious, but in the next instant, it occurred to her that they had all done the same thing, blamed the house as the culprit, as if it had been in on what had happened there. For the pointlessness of this to be so clear now, she wondered how it had been lost on her to begin with.

"Blame things on people," Mira said. "That's how blame was meant to work."

Kat paused, then looked at Mira with a half smile. "We're up to our ears in guilt." They walked past a Subaru that had tried to cross the median to turn around but had gotten stuck in the soggy dip in the center. The driver, an overweight teenage girl, stood by crying while two men, almost parallel to the ground, leaned into the car's back fender, digging their toes into the soil for leverage, as a third man in the driver's seat gunned the gas pedal.

Mira looked back at Kat. "You're the only blameless one."

Kat shook her head and smoothed her hand down over her face. "I knew you were in the house with Ray."

"I know."

When she wanted to, Kat could stare as intently as anyone Mira knew, so that you were certain she wasn't looking at your mouth or the lines of your brow or the air in front of your face, but your eyes. Next to hers, the stares of others could seem muted, as if they were coming at you through a pane of glass. So Kat shot Mira one of those dead-on stares and said, "I think the guilt's all evened out." And about this, Mira decided she was right.

When they got back, Aron and Felissa were sitting on the hood of the flatbed, their feet dangling down onto the windshield. Felissa's hair was pulled around in front of her. She braided it as they watched.

Mira hiked herself into the truck to check in on Ray. He was fiddling with the CB channels.

"Spooky, huh?" Ray said as she shifted into the seat, which was shiny black vinyl and greasy, as if it had just been coated with Armor All.

He was trying to make out the overlapping banter over the CB: "Could aim the thing at the cops, too." "... scrawny little pissant ..." "Navy Seal ..." "Thing's got a trigger on it." "... seen a ghost ..." "Cars backed up three miles by now ..."

As Mira listened, she spotted a metal emery board with a pink handle nudged halfway in the seat crack. It was powdered with fingernail dust.

"Woman's his estranged wife." "... blasted kook..." "TV movie..." "Got a tanker full of vitamin D milk." "... sicko hippie..." "Damn Straight..."

After a few minutes, Ray glanced in his outside mirror and did the closest Mira had ever seen to a real-life double take.

"What?" Mira asked.

"Kat's doodling on the house."

Mira stepped out and walked around the front of the truck. Kat was sitting cross-legged on the roof of the pickup, about a foot away from the house, facing it, her oil paints at her feet.

Mira walked closer. In the bottom left corner of the rectangle was a life-size cat resting on its hind legs, front paws gracefully placed before it. Kat had used white for its fur, so that against the yellow background of the house, it looked calico. The cat had a pretty mouth, a sliver of glossy red, and lazy avocado-colored eyes.

Mira said up toward her, "What's the artist's take on this?"

Kat jerked her head around as if she hadn't heard Mira coming, but she seemed pleased. She stuck her pencil-thin paintbrush between her teeth, pointed her chin toward the sky, and said in a generic European accent, "Self-portrait."

Just then, Ray stepped out of his truck. "It's over." He paused to trace a buzz to a helicopter overhead. "They cut the power." The toenail woman in the Acura let out a huge crescendoing laugh that seemed to bounce out of her car window and become part of the late-morning wind.

———

It took another hour for the cops to disperse and wave the traffic through. Back on their way, three hours after they had stopped, Felissa was in Aron's truck and Kat was back with Mira. Kat fumbled with the CB for a clear channel. A man identified as "Flattop Blacktop" said, "Umpteen jillion Arkansans got no TV or AC."

As they passed the mass of deadened power lines, Kat repeated the word *umpteen* in her head until it sounded like it came from a crooner singing in an unintelligible language, a lovely rhythmic note, worthy of repetition.

 _Fifteen_

They were idling on a two-lane road a mile outside of Mims, waiting for a skinny kid to recover the mattress that had just double-back-flipped off his truck bed. Aron had gotten out to give him a hand.

If Mira had closed her eyes, forgotten about the heat, she still would have known it was summer. The buzz of a thousand insects you never see, the tick of giant crop sprinklers, and the summer wind, the barely there sound of soft, pliable leaves tossing around, like the sound of hair being brushed.

The mattress secured, they started toward town. The road sliced through fields of ankle-high soybean plants, the rows as straight as church pews. They drove past the marble sculpture of Shelton Mims. An orange-vested man on a ladder leaned into its torso, scouring the crevices. Mira nudged Kat, who was half-asleep.

"No wake, please." Her eyes were still closed.

"Look, Shelton's getting his annual cleaning." Kat smiled faintly without opening her eyes.

To avoid traffic and the sagging branches of oak trees that lined the main road into town, they took a right onto old Highway 21; there was no new Highway 21, as far as Mira knew. This took them past a stretch of new houses on plots barely bigger than the houses themselves. Each one had the same look, prefab and aluminum-sided, yard heavily ornamented: a wooden bird on a stick, its wings twirling like propellers, a flock of plastic ducks waddling in single file, a plywood cutout of a fat woman bending down to weed.

A few minutes later, in the sleepy midafternoon light, they found Kearney, the Scangas, Wayne Gaar, and half a dozen men from his crew standing in a semicircle on the plot of fifteen acres, the rest sitting on open tailgates. Mira didn't see Liz.

The fresh concrete-slab foundation, just slightly larger than the dimensions of the house, sat a hundred feet off the road and rose to a few inches above the topsoil. A spray-painted *X* marked the center, as if it were a landing pad waiting for a helicopter to descend to ground level, the hydraulic jacks already positioned along the edge like control towers.

The lot was surrounded by profitable rice plantations, but the previous owner had left his land fallow, didn't care to fool with cultivation, the Realtor had said. The only planting he had done had been in a single greenhouse. Its corrugated plastic had since been stripped away, leaving just the aluminum frame, a half-cylinder skeleton arcing toward the ground as if still connected to its other half, submerged in the soil. He hadn't neglected the land, though, having bush-hogged it twice a year. And smack in its middle, just thirty feet behind where the foundation now lay, he had overseen the construction of a pond. Shaped to scale like the state of Arkansas and about as large as an Olympic-size pool, it was the only one like it in existence, he had boasted at the closing.

Ray was out of his cab and talking to Wayne, but he stood so he could see the road. Mira knew he was watching for Liz. Maybe there had been a crisis at work. A botched installation. Maybe a garage door had malfunctioned, closed on a car just halfway out. Maybe some truants had gotten ahold of a universal remote and were terrorizing Liz's service area. Or maybe she had decided there was no point in coming after all.

Kearney reached for Mira's door handle before she had come to a complete stop. "Hey, kiddos." He leaned down to kiss her on the cheek, fingered the bandage there. "You two get in a fight?" He seemed anxious, overly so, and Mira knew he was looking for signs of the way things had turned out, as if he needed them to know how to act, or what to do next.

The Scangas walked up, Jack looking seamless as always, the immaculate man that he was. His clothes were as well coordinated as a four-year-old's romper suit. Rhinetta seemed to share his like of order and spotlessness, though hers came across as being learned, his more innate.

"Glad that's out of the way, huh?" Jack touched his cheek to Mira's, his thin lips kissing only the air.

Rhinetta leaned up and gave Mira a quick hug, then gave Kat an identical one. "Happy housewarming." She handed Mira a burlap welcome mat rolled up and tied with a ribbon. Her smile revealed an unfortunate amount of gum above her top teeth. Mira was happy for her that she at least had healthy gums, shiny and pink.

Wayne Gaar stepped up and reached out his hand, which felt scratchy and tough when Mira shook it, like it was made of beef jerky. "You're hired," he said, greeting her in his friendly way. On his forearm was a tattoo she hadn't noticed before. It was meant to be an eagle, but his skin had sagged just enough to distort it, like a design on a deflated balloon. The eagle had taken on the look of a droopy butterfly, its wings rounded and its beak like a nub.

"How's she look?" At first, Mira thought Wayne meant Lila.

Then she realized he was staring at the foundation, smiling, his head bobbing up and down. "Guaranteed for the lifetime of the house."

Jack nodded in sync with Wayne. "Can't beat that."

Wayne held a small megaphone to his mouth and aimed it toward his crew. "Let's get this egg laid." He walked up and placed a hard hat sideways on Ray's head. "Enough dawdling, son." Then he walked over to Aron, who was standing off to the side with Felissa. The three of them stood there for a minute, Wayne shaking Felissa's hand while Aron held her other one. Then Wayne led Aron toward the house with his arm over Aron's shoulder, talking and gesturing as they went. Felissa laid her suitcase in the grass and straddled it, ready to watch.

A huge man with long hair tucked under his hard hat had just finished unhooking the chains from the base of the house. Aron and Wayne stood on either side of the foundation, the rest of the crew looking on as Ray got into his cab. He reversed the truck over the concrete slab, edging back steadily, giving it just the right amount of gas to force the hind wheels up on top of the foundation, which was a few inches high, then let off the next instant, his head swiveling the whole time between the two side mirrors. When the front of the house was lined up with the foundation, Ray came to a stop and idled while Wayne walked around to see if the house was centered. When he was satisfied that it was, Wayne waved a thumbs-up to Ray.

Mira heard the rumble of a car on the unpaved road that for now would serve as the driveway. A white minivan with a company logo on the side door was parking behind the line of pickups already there. It was Liz. As she started toward them, though her face was a blur, Mira could tell right away that she had short hair. Mira had hoped for long. She had always felt less threatened by such women.

She knew this was irrational, even ugly, and had never admitted it aloud.

Just as he got out of his cab, Ray spotted Liz and started toward her. She saw him, too, and adjusted her shirt at her waist, then ruffled the hair at her forehead. Standing off to the side about thirty feet from where Ray and Liz met, Mira just watched. Kat was with her, so for her benefit, Mira tried to disguise her stare at first, pretending that she couldn't figure out who the woman was. This lasted a few seconds, until Mira gave up the pretense and gawked as openly as if it were a scene being played out just for her. She tried thinking of it this way, tried to imagine it as a clip from a movie—her father had once suggested this as a means of detachment—but it didn't work. She still felt like herself, and all she saw were Ray and Liz, no acting to it.

Liz was smallish, came up just to his neck, so when they hugged, her feet left the ground and swung a bit. He set her down, then cupped one hand around her side, combed his other through her hair and kissed her, cocking his head down and to the side. She hooked a finger into his belt loop and pulled him closer, then seemed to wipe away his mustache of sweat with her forefinger. They both smiled at this. The way they fell into these tiny gestures, as if they had exchanged them a thousand times, made each one seem perfectly natural and familiar, but somehow not routine. Mira decided to be happy for them, as much as a person can decide such a thing.

Kat stood with her sister, not saying anything, as if she was letting Mira have her moment. Then, when Mira finally broke her stare, Kat hooked their arms and led the way toward the rest.

The crew was almost done inserting steel beams in the holes that had been drilled for the original move. Wayne was bent down with his hands on his knees, leaning over a young guy and a middle-aged woman as they slid the beams into position. He was coaching, miming their next move.

Mira recognized Ray's walk as he came up behind them. He started fumbling out Liz's introduction before Mira had turned around. She and Liz said the ordinary things: "Nice to meet you." "You, too. Lovely house." "Thanks, prime acreage." "Yes." Mira could tell Ray was uncomfortable. His eyes seemed sort of glazed, and he nodded during gaps in the small talk, as if to force things along. She wanted to reassure him, let him know it was okay, more okay than she had expected it would be, because Kat was there with her, close enough for Mira to smell her fruity shampoo, and Kearney was nearby, his green eyes, just like her own, half-squinting from the glare of the pastel sky. She wanted to tell Ray this, because it was true, but all she could do was smile.

Mira had imagined Liz to be beautiful, and she was. Her glossy brown hair was cut short all over, which served her well because her face carried all the weight. Her dark eyes almost matched her hair, and she had the kind of nose that put all other noses to shame. Her teeth were oddly small, but as white and straight as piano keys, and Mira got a good look at them because Liz couldn't stop smiling.

Wayne motioned for Ray to come over, and Mira was relieved when Liz turned her attention to the move, content to stand silently with the rest as they watched. A pair of crewmen perched next to each of the jacks, one with a steady eye on the gauges and steel beams, another watching for signs from Wayne. The low rumble of the jacks grew to a slightly higher pitch as the house was lifted off the flatbed.

The levitation seemed less real to Mira now than it had the first time around, more like a magic trick. She wasn't sure why. She thought of a slumber party she had been to once. In what she and her friends had called "a séance"—none of them had any real idea what such a thing was—seven or eight of them had placed two fingers from each hand under the skinniest girl at the party, who was lying down. When the call was made, they lifted her a foot off the floor. Thinking about it now, Mira no more understood how they had managed it than she had at the time.

When Lila was about two feet above the flatbed, Ray inched the truck forward, leaving the house suspended in midair, only the beams supporting it. Once the truck was out of the way, the hum of the jacks died down as they relaxed to lower the house squarely onto its foundation.

An hour later, after it was in place and the jacks had been wheeled back a few feet, Wayne announced that a dedication was in order. He walked to the cab of his truck and got a stack of cone-shaped paper cups and three bottles of sparkling cider. Mims was in a dry county.

"Huddle up." He waved two bottles in one hand, one in the other, like bowling pins, Wayne a clown about to juggle. He assured Mira that there would be no extra charge for the cider, then led them to the front right corner of the house. When everyone was there, he held his hand up for silence.

"It's fitting here to give a nod to the ancients, who held the belief that the sacrifice of a youthful virgin to the gods ensured the stability of their new dwellings. It was a ritual, or a sacrament, that type." Wayne paused, partly to dig two fingers into his shirt pocket, partly for effect.

He went on, the cigarette in his mouth wiggling: "Now, being that we have only one God to appease, and being that I'm not in the business of human sacrifice, a coin should suffice." He displayed a glossy penny on his palm for a few seconds—"Never been circulated," he said—then balanced it on his blackened thumbnail and flicked it onto the concrete slab. It bounced, then landed just to the left of center. "May this house stay safe from all catastrophes." Wayne inserted another dramatic pause, then added, "Man-made or otherwise."

After a practice swing, he pulled one of the bottles back over his shoulder and slammed it into the corner of the house. It burst into a fizzy spray, and Mira felt a tingle around her ankles from the cider or glass—she wasn't sure which. Wayne opened the first of the other two bottles and everyone lined up, each for half a cup.

The cider served, the crowd of twenty or so sipped and stared at Lila like sophisticates at an art opening, loose-tongued from chardonnay. Rhinetta mumbled something to Jack about liking the dentils, which she called "unusual." Wayne asked Mira if she would serve as a reference for future clients, maybe give him a blurb for next year's Yellow Pages. Mira overheard Aron tell Kearney that they would be out again the next day to anchor the house, seal the holes left from the steal beams. Kat was talking to one of the crewmen, who, it turned out, was the older brother of a friend of hers. Ray was working hard with big gestures and wide eyes to describe something to Liz, maybe telling her about the harpoon guy.

They were facing west, into the sun, so the front of the house was in shadow, a spray of rusty light coming from behind it. The scene looked like a doctored photo, the familiar background replaced by a silk screen of a lone silo on scantily wooded delta. It was like seeing your face on someone else's body. In this case, it looked different, but not in a bad way, and Mira knew that if her father were here, he would approve. She figured he would find

Wayne as endearing as she did. They would get to talking about the overlap between the contracting and house-moving businesses. Wesley would appreciate Wayne's improvised ceremony, and when he would say so, Helen—if she were here—would snap back at him in her charismatic way, then hold his stare an extra second and smile with her eyes, not giving away too much, just enough to let him know that she was only playing her role, not to take her too seriously. And Wesley would read her just right. He would swing his elbow into her back like he had always done and smile until she couldn't help but do the same.

Declining a refill of cider, Jack Scanga cupped Mira's elbow and told her to stop by the office anytime. She noticed that the button-down collar of his striped shirt had been left unbuttoned and wondered if this was intentional, and if not, how both of them had overlooked it. Rhinetta said she and Jack would have them over for dinner soon.

Mira looked around for Aron to say good-bye. He and Felissa were crouched in the grass, their faces just a foot away from a small anthill.

"This one's got some cargo." Felissa pointed at an ant a few inches from the hill.

In between laughs, Aron said in their direction, "Anybody got a magnifying glass?"

Mira stayed close to Kat and Kearney so that when Ray and Liz left, along with the rest, she could just be part of the collective good-bye, settle for a flicker of eye contact. And she guessed Ray was thinking the same thing, because instead of trying to get her alone or shoot her an important look, he just waved in tandem with Liz, then walked away, his his hand pressed into the small of his wife's back.

A half hour later, just after the last truck had pulled back onto the road, it was Kat who decided what they would do next.

"I'm wishin' to go fishin'."

Kearney shot Mira a sideways glance, then looked back at Kat. "You've never liked fishing."

"That's funny," Kat said, " 'cause I've never been fishing."

"Do you still have Dad's rods?" Mira asked.

"In my contraband closet."

Mira could remember a dozen times hearing her mother tell Kat that fishing wasn't part of the DeLand tradition. Knowing that the no-fishing rule had nothing to do with tradition and everything to do with Reverend Bleecher, Mira had once asked for a rundown on what the tradition was exactly. For this, her mother had given Mira a half-serious slap on her twenty-one-year-old calf as she climbed into the backseat of the Scamp.

As they walked toward the car, Kearney steered Mira out of Kat's earshot. "Anything you need to tell me?"

Mira cupped her hands like parentheses around her mouth. "There's nothing else to tell."

"Else?" he repeated. Mira took his hand, swinging it in semi-circles as she quickened their pace to catch up with Kat.

"Can I drive?" Kat asked once they were at the car.

"I don't know if that's a good idea with the K car. It's a fairly specialized machine."

"We'll keep the manual handy," Kat said.

Mira walked around the back of the car, noticed the Jesus fish, a new addition to the end of his trunk. They all sat in the front seat, Kearney in the middle. Kat drove.

"Notice anything?" Kearney waved his flattened hand in front of him.

"You drive a dorky car," Kat said.

"It's so dorky, it's cool. It takes me full circle." He pointed at the windshield and side windows.

"New tint?" Mira asked.

"Just had it installed the other day. It's a prototype one of Dad's clients sent me, self-adjusting to the sun, like the eyeglasses. The guy calls it Antisquint Tint. Just found a manufacturer for it."

"Dad would be giddy," Kat said.

"So somebody from your school left a message on Dad's machine," Kearney said to Mira. "A Martin something."

"It's Marcus. What did he say?"

"One of those 'Just called to see how you're doing' deals. I saved it for you."

"Did you tell him she's working for an escort service?" Kat snorted out a laugh.

They heard a siren and a second later saw red lights approaching. "Okay," Kearney said, "what's the procedure?"

"Check rearview for cars." Kat positioned her hands at ten and two. "Activate right turn signal, apply brake for gradual slowdown, gently steer toward shoulder, come to complete stop."

"You made that up," Mira said.

Kearney gave her thigh an affectionate pat. "Nice driving, Tex." The ambulance whined by.

At Kearney's house, Kat and Mira waited in the car while he went inside. Kat stayed in driving position, making unnecessary adjustments to the mirrors, skimming her palms around the wheel.

"So where should we bed down tonight?" Kat asked.

Mira was carving designs into the velour upholstery with her fingernails, then smoothing over them. "You call it."

"I think we should stay in Lila." Kat flashed her a smile, then simulated a lane change.

"We could do pallets to sleep on," Mira said.

"Mom taught me a good pallet technique."

Then Kearney came out with three Zebco rods and reels and an army green tackle box that Mira thought she recognized. He put all this in the backseat, rolling down a window to make room for the rods.

Mira paused before opening her door for him. "We're thinking the three of us should stay at the house tonight, break it in."

Kearney seemed a little surprised, but okay with the idea. "Christen it."

"Reinvent it," Kat added.

"Or something," Mira said. "We can order pizza. Do you have stuff for three pallets?"

Kearney nodded that he did, then went back inside. A couple of minutes later, he came out with a stack of pillows and blankets resting on his head. He stepped onto a railroad tie that separated the driveway from a bed of cedar chips, then tiptoed along it as if on a balance beam. After a few feet, he let his fake smile fade into an exaggerated look of concentration, then slowly let go of the blankets, floating his arms out beside him. Kat and Mira played along, yelling spectator and commentator lines: "Exquisite form." "Simple yet elegant." "Go for the gold." "We love you, Kearney." "Watch that dismount."

They parked just in front of Lila and walked around on the left side. Mira noticed through the plastic that one of the side windows had broken somewhere along the drive back.

She looked over at Kearney and lifted her eyebrows as if to ask him if he was getting spooked yet. After a pause, he shrugged in a way that seemed to say he was just fine.

They walked to the pond out back and onto the pier that extended over what would be western Arkansas. The tangle of lures in the tackle box looked like discarded earrings. Mira chose an alien-looking silver fish with metallic gold strands hanging the length of its body.

As it turned out, Mira was the best caster of the three of them, but no one got their line more than twenty feet past the pier. Kat didn't have the timing down, so her line kept releasing behind her, the lure catching in the weeds on the bank. Kearney released too late, his lure slapping into the water just a few yards away.

After they had all cast out as far as they could—Mira cast Kat's for her—they waited. Kearney started whistling the theme from *The Andy Griffith Show*.

"Pipe down," Mira whispered. "You're gonna scare the fish away."

"Are we even sure he stocked this thing?" Kearney asked.

"We'll get the effect anyway," Kat said.

Within a minute, Kearney's floater bobbed up and down. Kat squealed for him to reel it in. When he tried, there was no more tension on the line. He cast again.

Kat began to reel in. "I'm gonna reposition."

Kearney chastised her. "You're not gonna get it far enough out."

She faked a pout and recited a line from her script from Mims's birthplace. "The family's estate—strike that—the family's inheritance was divided among the children, except for the only son, or youngest son, whatever, who had been estranged from the family since the mother's death."

"Better brush up," Mira said, keeping an eye on her line.

"Okay." Kearney looked toward Kat. "Just do what I do." He reeled in and cast again. Acting out as he spoke, he said, "Press button, pull back over shoulder to forty-five degrees, then release button as you briskly pull rod forward." His lure landed a car length from the pier.

"I see a predawn fishing show on ESPN 2 in your future," Kat said.

Unfazed, Kearney said, "You try as I talk you through it." As he repeated the steps, Kat cast out, her tongue probing the inside of her cheek. This time, her line flew past his and Mira's, about forty feet beyond the pier. When Mira started to applaud, Kat hushed her. For the next few minutes, without a word, their eyes locked on the floaters, the three of them holding a vigil for whatever fish might be willing to humor them. The only sound was the tiny splashing of water against the pilings below the pier.

Kat got the next bite. Something tugged her floater to just below the surface. "What do I do?" She spoke like a librarian, careful not to disturb.

"Tug to hook it," Mira said.

"Then reel it in easy," Kearney added.

"It's still there." Kat's rod was bent now, forming a comma. Conscious not to jerk the thing loose, she reeled patiently, her back arched a little, knees bent, the rod's handle digging into her stomach. They spotted the fish when it was still a foot or so underwater, the late-afternoon sun already picking up some of its iridescence. As she raised the fish above the surface, it buoyed back and forth as if its spine were elastic. Kat stepped back and lowered the rod so that the fish lay on the wood planks of the pier. It was about eight inches long, its body sliverlike, gills easing up and down like a slow pulse.

"What is it?" Kat asked.

Kearney bent down to just a foot away to examine it. "A bream." Kat smirked at his quick identification. "What?" Kearney asked. "I know what a bream looks like."

"Yeah, when it's fried and served with coleslaw," Kat said sweetly.

Mira squatted next to Kearney. "Maybe it's a perch."

There was a nice wind, enough to pucker the water's surface so that it looked like there was a current. For a second, with her eyes aimed down at the fish and the water swishing around them, Mira felt like they were moving. Looking in between the pier's wood planks, she could see where the water grew shallow. Fuzzy strands of green algae lolled back and forth like long hair in a pool. If she hadn't known it was algae, she would have thought it was beautiful.

"Or a bass," Kearney was saying as Mira looked back to the catch. Its scales were like sequins, reflecting the orange tint the sky had taken on.

"It's a fish," Kat said. "That'll do." The thing seemed to look up at them, its eye like a marble, navy blue and perfectly round. "Do fish blink?"

Kearney shook his head. "They don't have to underwater."

"What if it needs to blink?" Kat bent closer.

"Here." Mira leaned down and cupped her hand with water, then dribbled it over the fish's eyes. Its spaghetti-thin lips were parted slightly, revealing tiny rows of fish teeth.

Kat bent down so that her face was within a foot of the fish's. "I think she needs back in."

"We can't leave the hook in there." Mira looked at Kearney.

"What?"

"You're the aficionado," Kat said.

Kearney looked at Mira. "You've fished as much as I have."

"We should hurry," Kat said. Its gills seemed to shiver.

Still squatting, Mira waddled closer to the fish and peered into its small pink mouth to see what angle the hook had lodged at. With her thumb and forefinger poked just inside, she tugged the hook in the opposite direction as gently as she could manage. It slid right out.

"She thanks you." Kat skimmed a single fingertip along a stretch of its papery scales.

Then, with both hands, Mira picked the fish up. It slipped out once before she got a good grip, so Kearney and Kat cupped their hands underneath, spotting it. Mira held on until the fish was just below the surface of the sun-warmed water, then let go one finger at a time. The thing fanned its body back and forth, wiggling away, out of sight, leaving the three of them squatting knees-to-chin on the pier, waiting to see what happened next.